William Wallace Faris

The Children of Light

William Wallace Faris

The Children of Light

ISBN/EAN: 9783337253844

Printed in Europe, USA, Canada, Australia, Japan

Cover: Foto ©Andreas Hilbeck / pixelio.de

More available books at **www.hansebooks.com**

The Fletcher Prize Essay,

1877.

THE

CHILDREN OF LIGHT.

BY

REV. WM. W. FARIS.

"Ye are all the Children of Light." — 1 Thess. v. 5.
"Walk as Children of Light." — Eph. v. 8.

BOSTON:

ROBERTS BROTHERS.

1877.

Cambridge:
Press of John Wilson & Son.

TO

MY FATHER,

CONTENTS.

Part Fourth.

WALKING IN THE LIGHT. (Christian Conduct.)

Part Fifth.

WORKING IN THE LIGHT. (Christian Labor.)

This then is the Message

WHICH WE HAVE HEARD OF HIM, AND DECLARE UNTO YOU,

THAT

GOD IS LIGHT,

AND IN HIM IS NO DARKNESS AT ALL.

IF WE SAY THAT WE HAVE FELLOWSHIP WITH HIM, AND WALK IN DARKNESS, WE LIE, AND DO NOT THE TRUTH:

BUT IF WE WALK IN THE LIGHT, AS HE IS IN THE LIGHT, WE HAVE FELLOWSHIP ONE WITH ANOTHER,

AND

THE BLOOD OF JESUS CHRIST HIS SON CLEANSETH US FROM ALL SIN.

1 John i. 5-7.

THE CHILDREN OF LIGHT.

LIGHTS AND SHADOWS:

A SURVEY.

"The morning cometh; and also the night." — ISA. xxi. 12.

THERE are some ten millions of communicants in the Christian churches of the United States. That is to say: there is this vast multitude of people among us who profess to have received an invaluable gift from Jesus Christ, and who have sworn to serve Him as their King.

Here is a host of men and women who daily take their dearest joys direct from the King's hand; whose exemption from the bitter fruits of their own misdeeds is due alone to His matchless grace; and who fully and fondly expect from Him eternal bliss, upon warrant of the covenant which He has executed, sealed, and delivered to their keeping: —

" If thou shalt confess with thy mouth the Lord Jesus, and shalt believe in thine heart that God hath raised Him from the dead, thou shalt be saved."

" Whosoever shall call upon the name of the Lord, shall be saved."

All these, therefore, are attached to their King by ties of love, and devoted to His interests from motives of gratitude. As, in an earlier day, one like them said : —

" For the love of Christ *constraineth* us ; because we thus judge, that if One died for all, then were all dead ; and that He died for all, that they which live should not henceforth live unto themselves, but unto Him which died for them, and rose again."

One would suppose, then, that this King, Jesus, could nowhere now lack partisans to defend His honor, or adherents to push His claims. One would imagine that to decry this King, or to oppose His cause, must be an undertaking attended with some instant hazard. And one would expect that, as vapor rises from the sea, so spontaneously and unceasingly there should arise from the gladdened hearts of all these millions, over the whole land, a huge cloud of earnest and eloquent testimony to His merits and His gifts ; and that, like some pent-up torrent, it would burst out upon the nations in an overwhelming flood; a testimony so joyous and eager, so outspoken and aggressive, so vigorous and so vast, that, like a marvel or a miracle, it must compel the attention of mankind !

Napoleon Bonaparte is long since dead, and his best gifts to men are now but brilliant dreams and urns of ashes; yet there are still many who will avenge an insult to his memory upon the spot. Washington is dead; yet there are thousands now who are both keenly sensitive to any dishonoring mention of him, and active in defending and developing the heritage which he bequeathed us. Christ still lives. His legacy is beyond all price and secure from all decay. The success of His work, unlike that of Washington, is inwoven with the honor of His name. His warfare presses and calls for reinforcements. His harvest fields are ripening to decay, whereat hearts ache and join the cry, till it echoes and re-echoes everywhere, "Send forth more laborers into the harvest;" while His redeemed stand near, numerous and able, catching from the Master's lips the words, "Go work."

With what vigor, then, should we suppose His warfare would be pressed, His harvest gathered! With what rapidity should we expect to see His gifts of healing scattered and accepted! With what promptness should we expect to find reproach or calumny against the name of Jesus caught up and hurled back upon the defamer, and opposition to His kindly work conquered and consigned to ignominy! With what quenchless ardor should we expect to see the standard of the cross borne forward, and hear its virtues heralded in the ears of men who are dying for want of the saving word and the healing vision! And especially, at the very outset indeed, we should certainly expect to find all these Christians, with a rigid and loving fidelity, cherishing the spirit and following the example

of their Master in discarding and abhorring
sin of every sort, and in maintaining purity of
heart and life ; in order that, at the very least, no
. act or indulgence of theirs might mar their own
joy, subject the King's name to contumely, and
retard His redeeming work.

Such are the pleasing expectations which it
would seem but just to indulge. What are the
facts ?

An impartial survey discloses almost nothing
of the kind, except in certain quarters and
within narrowly restricted limits. The words
of the evangel still hold good : —

"The harvest truly is plenteous, but the laborers
are few !"

"The children of this world are, in their generation,
wiser than the children of light."

The kingdom of light receives less vigorous
and less faithful service than the kingdom of
darkness.

There is, indeed, much unction among ministers of the Gospel. But the world, which
needs to be impressed, imputes this zeal to the

spirit of the minister's profession rather than to the emotion of his heart; nor is it possible, by any analysis, to determine the full extent to which this human factor enters. Moreover, some ministers are given to avarice, ambition, indolence. And, after giving due credit for the large and undoubted self-sacrifice which remains, it must still be said that the clergy are an official class supported in and for their work; and that they are but the very few " among the thousands of Judah."

It is true also that there is an occasional and sporadic lay activity. One by one, at intervals of generations and at distances of hundreds of miles, there arise a few devoted men whose infectious spirit is caught, and for a time is kept, by scores or hundreds in the immediate vicinity of each. And in almost every community there may be found at least one or two persons, often in the humbler walks of life, whose activity is similar in its quality and its results to that of these more influential laborers; while it not unfrequently occurs that, under

God, a whole church is indebted to this one or two for the greater part of its zeal and its success.

At rare times, also, one may come upon the path of a faithful and effective toiler for the Master, who has the happy knack of working unseen of men. Usually, perhaps, it is a woman. One seldom meets her. The world hears little of her. But there are those among the poor, the sick, the troubled, who know her cheering voice, and who learn to listen for her almost stealthy footstep. She is often able also to inspire, to direct, and even to organize the efforts of the less thoughtful and earnest, without permitting herself to be in any way thrust into public notice. Such persons command at once our admiration and our esteem; and all the more because of their rarity.

It is freely granted that much activity may be found in still other and diverse quarters. In the aggregate, its display is perhaps as large as all that has been named. But scrutiny detects an unconscious deception here. This work is

usually of an intermittent and a very ordinary
sort. The most of it is either the dead fruit of
habit, or a mere series of convulsive efforts produced by a succession of urgent appeals and
cutting rebukes. Such service has small claim
to honorable recognition.

Worthy of a better mention is the silent influence of a respectable minority of the Christian
host, mostly wives and mothers, whose speech
is in whispers to God in the closet and in patient
counsel to their young. The Christian spirit
proves pervasive in the homes of these women;
it exhales a fragrance which fills the place, and
it rests like a benediction on the heads of all
who enter there. With them we may associate
some men, quiet persons, often poor in this
world's goods; humble mechanics, unlettered
or diffident farmers, moderately successful trades-
men, professional men of a retiring disposition.
Their influence is felt, but also it is restricted.
There is a degree of unvoiced devotion displayed
in their lives; but their name is not legion, their
work is not spirited, and their achievements are
not great.

Remark may also be made upon the prevalence of that phase of Christian conduct which exhibits regard for the common decencies of life, for the rights of others, and for the claims of the needy. This, however, is but the remote result of centuries of Christian teaching and endeavor: it is chiefly the product of other ages than our own. The habit is almost universal in Christendom. It marks the present terminus of the pathway of *light* through the ages, whose departure was from Mount Calvary, or, more remotely, from the altar at the gate of Eden. It is scarcely to be credited either to the devoutness or to the exertions of the present generation of Christians, but the rather to its acquiescence and acceptance. As a rule the Christians of to-day, and many of the world with them, only fall in with the tide of civilization which has been rolled upward and is now borne on by other hands than theirs. For, let it be remembered, that which is here claimed and which is indeed a pleasing fruit of our religion, is simply the habit of Christian decency, not the vigorous

1*

virtue of the Christian life. The eminent godliness of demeanor which the times demand and
which compels the respect of men as the unques-
tionable product of Grace, is not so common.

Even this outward decency is often wanting.
The sensitive ear of the lover of God's house is
pained by the frequent report of some petty
misdemeanor, or some grave crime, committed
by a professed follower of Jesus; so that fresh
stains are fixed upon the Christian name by
those who wear it.

It is thus that the pleasing anticipations with
which we set out upon our survey are doomed
to disappointment. The rigid fidelity and the
rapt devotion which we expect, are found " only
in certain quarters and within narrowly restricted limits." Beyond what has been men-
tioned there is — nothing; nothing to compel
the attention of the unobservant to the fact that
Jesus *lives;* nothing adequate to overcome the
inertia of human lethargy and human scepticism
concerning the great needs and truths of life;
nothing to give to the careless and the vicious

such constant and vivid warning of their ruin as should force them to pause and think.

It is not intended to deny that the aggregate *result* of Christian work is large. Many blessed and glorious ends are achieved : their number cannot be reckoned, and their value is beyond estimation. The support of the American Bible Society and its countless auxiliaries, of the various Tract and Missionary Associations, and of hundreds of diverse schemes and agencies of Christian education and Christian charity; and the maintenance and care, together with their Sabbath schools, of more than fifty thousand Christian churches, — attended by a growth more rapid in the aggregate than that of our population ; wherein are involved a total annual outlay of millions of dollars and the steady toil of hosts of workers : these things exhibit the marvellous power of *Grace* as it operates through such frail and unreliable materials as are seen, to a great extent, to compose the church of Christ ; and they exhibit also the wisdom of *Providence*, which gathers to such useful ends so many rills of influence flowing from many sources and springing from various motives. Praise is due to God in that He is able and is pleased to accomplish so much through lives so frail, hands so weak, and will so feeble as humanity ordinarily offers in His service.

So much of the outlay named is from motives of display, so much of it is drawn from unwilling hands, and so much is unmade which might justly have been looked for; so much of the work performed was organized in former times and is now carried on, under God, largely by its own momentum, while so much more is wanting which might easily be supplied; that, except as to the classes to whom allusion has been made, the measure of recognition due to man's fidelity, vigilance and zeal, is scant indeed! Much is accomplished and a gigantic work is carried forward measurably well, only because God is able to work effectively through even a sluggish current of Christian life. It remains that the human elements of the forces of righteousness might offer Him an agency for the accomplishment of immensely more, by unanimously laying a resolute will, a glowing heart, and a willing hand on the Redeemer's altar.

We looked to see a marvel of devotion. We find it wanting; and we find instead — a miracle of divine management. The multitude of the redeemed are found to be characterized rather by indifference and inconsistency, than by the purity of life and the vigilance and vigor of service which were to be anticipated. And especially does it appear that the alert and partisan aggression in Jesus' name which a lethargic world requires, is wofully restricted.

Were it not so, hosts of prevailing ills would have hidden their heads ere this. What cannot ten millions of people accomplish! In a total population of but forty millions, ten millions of intelligent adults — united, resolute and eager in this personal partisanship, aided by the sympathies of many whom certain lines exclude from their company, permitted in every emergency to employ the power of the Throne which is behind all thrones and the Wisdom which is behind all thought — must .inevitably infuse their thought into public opinion and civil law so far that manifest injustice or fraud, and evident dishonor, insult or opposition to Jesus, save among the openly and defiantly vicious, would become impossible because so exceedingly unpopular. It were in our power, without in the least infringing on the rights of others, to make profanity, blasphemy, fraud, indecent speech, and even irreverence and open violation of the Sabbath, so damaging to those known to be guilty of them, that these crying sins would soon cease to be exhibited in open day, or to be screened or winked at by law or custom. Injustice, extortion, oppression, bribery, would sink from sight. Want would be almost unknown. And Peace would rest upon the nation.

Our entire population would soon be divided into two ˌdistinct and opposing classes — the friends of righteousness on the one hand, and the recklessly ungodly and the vicious on the other. Their conflicts at the polls, in the court room and in the halls of legislation, would be frequent and often fierce, with one unvarying result, — vice would be put in stern and utter subjection on every occasion.

Further: the evangelistic success to be achieved by the prevalence throughout the Christian host of such a character and habit, is beyond conception. Every infidel who screens himself behind the shortcomings of Christians would be stripped of his excuses and his arguments at once. Hosts of the indifferent would be daily subjected to awakening influences, if only from example, which they would be powerless to resist, — albeit they might, and many doubtless would, make final and deliberate choice of evil in the full light of truth. In fine, this gospel light would quickly penetrate to the remotest corner of the land, to the darkest quarters of our cities, to the hearts of all the prejudiced and the indifferent; and the division of men, for and against our King, would be precipitated in an incredibly brief time. Our evangelistic work would be completed, so far as it concerns our own present population; while the labor of the future would be prepared for, and work in foreign fields would be pushed forward, as never before.

It is apparent, then, that there is pressing need of two distinct yet closely related fruits of the Spirit of God : —

First: There is required the general prevalence of a godly atmosphere, generated by the character of Christians, and by the god-likeness of their conduct in the affairs of daily life. The " light of men " should shine among men, through them who receive it, and who are therefore divinely termed " lights in the world," and " children of light."

Mere Christian decency will not suffice. It gives no adequate illumination. The world is so far able to match us in this accomplishment, that our display of it yields no convincing testimony to the power of our risen Lord to create men anew and to inspire them to righteousness. What they see they ascribe to the mere teaching and example of the dead Jesus, and these they claim to be the heritage of the world at large, not of Christ's kingdom in particular. There must be such eminent virtue as shall pass the power of Satan to produce, or of men to imitate.

It is not cant we want, nor sanctimony, bigotry, or spiritual pride; for they have not this origin, nor do they produce these fruits. What we want is a natural and real presence of the spirit of Jesus in the hearts of His followers, in power, setting them apart from men, not in the conscious superiority of pride, but by the simple force of that sweetness of temper, that rigid, constant and natural uprightness of conduct, that fulness of brotherly love, which marked the Nazarene. We want nothing that savors of hypocrisy or gloom, or that hides its origin in darkness; nothing unworthy of the children of light; nothing that is not pure, that will not endure the scrutiny of that searching *Light* which beams full upon the world.

Second: After this, there is crying need of aggression. The lesson which the sweet example of the Christian shall create, needs to be thrust home. Appeal must be made to men. Righteousness is to be infused throughout the realms of law, society and commerce. The present schemes of Christian evangelism, culture and charity, call loudly for reinforcements; and there is ever need that new schemes be set on foot. We want good soldiers of Jesus Christ, wearing the "armor of light" and wielding the sword of truth. We want men with consecrated tongues to speak, brains to devise, and purses to give, for Christ. In a word, we need a determined advance and a bold aggression all along the line, as well as a maintenance in righteousness of the ground already occupied.

When, now, in order to devise a remedy we seek to apportion blame, we are met by a serious problem; so vast is our failure and so wide is its reach.

It is worthy of specific mention, however, that the class of Christians from which the most efficient aggression might be expected, is seldom heard from on the battle-field. This class is composed of stirring, successful merchants and manufacturers; farmers and traders of means, influence and large operations; prominent physicians; attorneys of extensive reputation; statesmen of note; men of letters; women who rule in society or who wield a facile pen; and all who are recognized as "leaders," whether to a great or small extent and whether in a wide or narrow sphere.

These are the people who, with others like them in every thing but their adherence to Christ, make the most noise in the world in general. They effect changes of laws, customs, ideas. They bear sway in society, in the court room, in the halls of legislation, in political organizations, in the centres of trade. Yet withal many, if not the most of them, seldom or never make personal appeal or personal exertion for Christ or for dying men. All the more honor to those of them who do!

This is not all. These people are industrious and successful — in work that suits them. In pushing selfish interests they are bold and energetic. Their fault lies deeper than their inaction in the Master's service: it lies in their all-absorbing selfishness. They are notably "conformed to this world." Their time, their talent, their means, their influence, are lavished on the altar of Vanity, while the altar of Christ stands bare !

He who has no time for thought upon or action in the great work of the church; who has neither time nor taste for devising means and measures for the elevation of the masses; no time to attend a religious convention, much less to elaborate a stirring and practical address for delivery there; no time to devise the founding or the fostering of churches, schools or charities, or the inauguration of reforms, yet has time to forecast the rise and fall of stocks and the fluctuations of trade; has hours and days to spend in anxious thought on railroad combinations or on political or commercial complications; until *Power* becomes his controlling thought, and Christ and humanity seem but the actors in a receding dream.

She who has no leisure and no gifts for teach-

ing in the Sabbath school or for direct endeavor
toward the elevation of the degraded, yet has
tact to win *Society* to her drawing-rooms, and
time by the day with which to respond to her
tyrant's exorbitant demands. Not subjecting
society to Christ and using it for Him, — as some
most nobly do, and as she might do with little visible change of habit, — but, surrendering herself
in degrading slavery to be swayed for the glory of
Mammon, she abuses God's good gifts until her
heart grows callous to appeal from the suffering
or in their behalf ; until her affections become
fastened and are frittered away upon the vani-
ties of the hour ; until her heart grows cold
toward Jesus himself, and her actions become
indistinguishable from those of His contemners
and His foes.

This is worldliness, — the blight of the church !
These Christians are walking as "children of
darkness and of the night." Their hearts have
become fixed on worldly things. They have
come to love worldly society, aims, fashion,
culture, small talk. Their mightiest efforts are

put forth, their keenest ardor is displayed, in the pursuit, the capture, and the momentary enjoyment of trifling ambitions light as air and unsubstantial as the bubble which delights the child. And loving these glittering, transient things so well, their lives unconsciously take on some of their changing hues and tints; but at the cost of piety, worth and usefulness.

Thus it is that they have grown worldly at heart, and have become conformed to this world in their lives. The world has crept in, and by necessary consequence their Christian life is dwarfed, sickly, and gasping for breath.

Something like this is the condition of many of our " ten millions " of communicants, — how many it is impossible to say. What wonder that the fruits of godliness are so scant!

Let there be no mistake. It is by no means meant to restrict this observation to those whose exalted position has made their ignoble career so prominent. The worldly Christians are not all after this order. There are also the indolent, who love worldly ease; the sordid, whose

canker is " the love of money ; " the vain and
giddy, whose religion seems as frothy and inane
as are their ordinary speech and behavior ; the
place-seekers in the church, — no petty host ; the
merely indifferent, who maintain an outward
respectability and are satisfied ; the wayward
and the careless, almost and sometimes quite
immoral ; and alas ! there are also some who
are stumbling, and some who have already
fallen, into manifest disgrace.

All these are walking " in darkness," their
eyes closed to the light ; while yet there ever
sounds in their heedless ears the entreaty of
their Lord to " walk even as He walked," to
maintain His honor and to advance His interests ; while yet there arise on every side the
cries of men in testimony that sin has wrecked
the race, and pleading for human help to rescue
souls from the ruins.

To all such comes the affectionate admonition
of the Saviour : —

"Let your light so shine before men."

And this voice of the Master wakes the

echoes of the Scriptures, so that the words come back again from every quarter: —

" Ye are all the children of light and the children of the day; we are not of the night, nor of darkness. Therefore let us not sleep, as do others. . . . For they that sleep, sleep in the night ; and they that be drunken are drunken in the night. But let us who are of the day be sober, putting on the breastplate of faith and love, and for a helmet the hope of salvation."

" The path of the just is as the shining light that shineth more and more unto the perfect day."

" But if we walk in the light as He is in the light, we have fellowship one with another. . . . "

" Walk as *children of light.*"

PART FIRST.

—◆—

COMING TO THE LIGHT.

(Christian Beginnings.)

———

" He that doeth truth cometh to the light." — John iii. 21.

2

I. Starting Out.

II. Locating the Light.

———

"Awake! thou that sleepest, and arise from the dead, and Christ shall give thee light." — Eph. v. 14.

I.

STARTING OUT.

"While ye have light, believe in the light, that ye may be the children of light." — JOHN xii. 36.

"Dost thou believe on the Son of God?" — JOHN ix. 35.

IS the reader a Christian? This question confronts us upon the very threshold of all converse, whether concerning the soul's safety hereafter, or its usefulness, honor and happiness here.

Jesus of Nazareth proclaims himself the life and the light of men.

He teaches: that "men love darkness rather than light, because their deeds are evil;" that by nature they are "the children of darkness," blinded by "the god of this world," and befogged in hopeless doubt as to truth, duty, and destiny; that they "walk in darkness," oppressed by guilt, beclouded by the exhalations of indwelling sin, stumbling as they go, and so doomed to plunge at last into a destiny of " blackness of darkness " — to be cast into " outer darkness," where shall be " weeping and gnashing of teeth."

This is, in part, His portraiture of the kingdom of darkness. It swallows up all mankind. There is no light, no valid hope of a bright future, no escape from the midnight gloom which has already settled down, or from the appalling doom in which it must issue — unless *light* appear from without.

In man's dire need the light appears. Whence is it? What is it?

We are told that, in the last analysis, " God is light, and in Him is no darkness at all."

But God is not said to be " the light *of men*," for he is invisible; so far His light is of no avail. Will God reveal Himself? There is already the revelation in nature; but neither does that include a remedy for the sin and death which were unknown when this revelation was made, nor can the eyes which sin has since bedimmed discern what was adapted only to the keen vision of a righteous soul. Shall there be a revelation adapted to the *sinner's* wants?

The Son of God comes. He assumes our nature. His human name is Jesus. He is " the Word of God," revealing Him — " God was *manifest* in the flesh." In Him the light becomes visible to mortal eyes. As He announces himself, He is " the light of the world," " the light of men."

His divine pity makes known God's love for us. His sacrificial death opens before us the path to forgiveness and reconciliation to God. His teaching and conduct make our duty doubly plain. His character exhibits the image we need to bear. His gift of the Holy Ghost, and the subordinate gifts of the Bible, the Church and the Sabbath, disclose the method of our recovery. And His promises guarantee *every thing* to the soul that will simply trust Him. The light has come! Man's want is met!

Accordingly, men are invited to Christ: —

" Look unto me, and be ye saved, all the ends of the earth."

"Awake! thou that sleepest, and arise from the dead, and Christ shall give thee light."

"While ye have light, believe in the light, that ye may be the children of light."

And the promises are : —

"Believe on the Lord Jesus Christ, and thou shalt be saved."

"He that believeth on the Son hath everlasting life."

"He that followeth me shall not walk in darkness, but shall have the light of life."

Unto this light our eyes are to be opened ; to it they are to be lifted ; we are to follow it, to commit ourselves unreservedly to its guidance. That is to say, it is necessary to the happiness, the usefulness, the *redemption* of men, that they "believe in the light," and so become "the children of light." Wherefore the question is thrust home upon the soul: "Dost thou believe on the Son of God?"

Is the reader a Christian? Even apart from the question of destiny involved, this matter is fundamental. It is impossible to "walk as children of light" except we be of their num-

ber. And it is in vain to suggest counsel looking toward such a walk while doubt hangs upon
the prior question of the "being."

Multitudes are oppressed by this doubt.
They may be Christians nevertheless. If so,
their destiny is secure. Mere doubt does not
exclude from heaven. But its presence bars
the way against almost all appeal. The promises lose their force with one who hesitates to
receive them to himself. The injunctions, exhortations, warnings and enticements of the
Scriptures, which are addressed in such abundance to and are possessed of so much power
over the Christian, are pointless for the soul
who knows not what he is, who is continually
leaping from pillar to post and from post to
pillar, unwilling or unable to take his place
either among God's people or among His enemies. Letters addressed to a citizen of heaven
are not accepted by the man who will not wear
the name. It is difficult to feed one who dan-
gles at the end of an elastic cord between
heaven and earth, or to reach with an urgent

message one who is ever restlessly passing and repassing from shore to shore of a great ocean.

The doubting Christian has no status. He has no certain consciousness. He knows not whether he be saint or sinner: messages for the one and the other slip by him in turn ungrasped. He knows not by what motives he may be influenced. He feels small interest in the delightful promises attached to the commands for Christian work. He has little heart for a service which presupposes a soul filled with joy over its assured redemption. In a word, his doubt cuts the sinews of his activity, bedims the joy that would prompt him to it, and dulls the edge of the warnings which crowd the path of his cowardly retreat. However it may fail to interfere with his final acquittal and redemption, it fatally mars his happiness and usefulness meanwhile.

Is the reader a Christian? This is the most momentous question which the soul will ever be called upon to answer. It is certainly worth while to pause in order to obtain a rational and decisive judgment as to one's standing before God and his eternal destiny. No one can afford to remain in doubt. Too much is at stake to warrant the indulgence of any peace or contentment while the doubt remains.

There is no need that doubt remain. There is nothing in the nature of the case to prevent the speedy attainment of a rational certainty. The conditions of the question are briefly, plainly, and repeatedly given. No tedious research, no painful process, is required. The Giver of salvation must lay its law alone. He has issued no uncertain or puzzling declarations to bewilder the judgment, but has said : " The word is nigh thee." If one come into a puzzled and bewildered state of mind, it must be because he has neutralized the force of God's simple words by mingling with them " the traditions of men." When these traditions are given a hearing, they produce a confusion of ideas, a misconception of the facts, and a refusal to receive to one's self the declarations meant for him. Bewilderment sets in at once upon

2*   c

this refusal, and the soul drifts helplessly out into the terrible fog of uncertainty. While also it is true that some, misguided by the same false light, are led by it to indulge a calm assurance and a serene contentment upon the supposition that they are Christians, when they certainly are not Christians. Is *the reader* a Christian?

1. Not all members of the church are the children of God. Christ said : —

"Not every one that saith unto me, 'Lord, Lord,' shall enter into the kingdom of heaven. . . . Many will say to me in that day, 'Lord, Lord, have we not prophesied in thy name, and in thy name cast out devils, and in thy name done many wonderful works?' And then will I profess unto them, 'I never knew you; depart from me, ye that work iniquity?'"

It is to be feared that many a professing Christian of our day, perhaps many a minister of the Gospel, will be addressed in these words at the judgment. The communion-roll of the church on earth affords no adequate evidence of one's standing before God. Nor do good works,

as a member or an officer of the church, avail:
" Not of works lest any man should boast."

A Christian was once called to see the wife of
an English clergyman, who lay apparently dying
far from home and her husband. Presuming
that she was a Christian, he merely quoted a
few texts of Scripture suitable to her as such, to
comfort her, then prayed with her and with-
drew. As he left the outer door, he heard her
bell ring. A moment later, he was overtaken
by a servant who in the lady's name asked him
back. Upon his return, she said : —

" Ah, sir ! I have no such peace and comfort
as you presume. *Do speak to me about the way
of salvation.* I have played the harmonium in
our church, kept a girls' class, presided over a
Dorcas society, and all that; but these things
fail to quiet my conscience in the prospect of
appearing before God."

This Scripture was named and dwelt upon:
" God so loved the world that He gave His only
begotten Son, that whosoever *believeth in Him*
should not perish, but have everlasting life." It

was sought to divert her attention from what she had done to Christ, that she might say —

> " I trust in what my Lord has done
> And suffered once for me."

The lady repeated the text to herself musingly several times, and said:

"I know that passage well; but I see there is something in it I have never observed before."

The Lord blessed the word and also raised her up. The *blood* brought peace to her conscience when all else had failed. She goes on with her works as before, but from quite different motives. Her church-membership " and all that " are not now in order to be saved, but because she is saved, and because, being saved, she desires to walk in the light.*

The inquiry is not, Is the man a church-member? but, "Dost thou believe on the Son of God?"

2. This is not a question of " experience," as the term is commonly used in the churches.

The experience is not a matter of observation;

* From " Life and Light."

it cannot furnish a test. Regeneration is God's work. It is wrought, not before men's eyes, but in the fathomless depths of the soul. It involves in its process the subtlest, the most secret workings of the heart. Comparisons of the " experience " reveal vast differences in different persons. One has no warrant for measuring himself by others : —

" For we dare not make ourselves of the number, or compare ourselves with some, that commend themselves ; but they, measuring themselves by themselves, and comparing themselves among themselves, are not wise. . . . But he that glorieth, let him glory in the Lord."

Many trust more in their experiences than in Christ. As a consequence when variations of feeling come, as they are sure to come, these people are plunged into doubt and distress. Religion is experimental ; but the experience has been erected *as a test* by man alone, and contrary to the tenor and the letter of the Word. The change wrought is instantaneous and vital, but the Scriptures are silent concerning the supposed necessity of its detection, as a matter of observation or of feeling, at the time of its occurrence or at any other time. Christ preached regeneration to Nicodemus when he was lethargic and self-confident. The moment he betrayed the dawning of interest and of a practical purpose, the Master skilfully turned the subject of discourse, saying :—

" As Moses lifted up the serpent in the wilderness, even so must the Son of Man be lifted up, that whosoever *believeth in Him* should not perish, but have eternal life."

In this form of discourse He continued ; nor did He once return to the matter of regeneration, or intimate the necessity of aiming at it as a separate end, or of trusting in the experience of it as an evidence of salvation. The drift is evident: it is for man to believe, for God to recreate. The necessity of regeneration is thundered in the ears of the careless and the self-righteous. But to the awakened soul comes this word: " Believe on the Lord Jesus Christ, and thou shalt be saved." And to the doubting disciple it is declared: " He that believeth that Jesus is the Christ *is* born of God."

The eyes are to rest only on the cross. Regeneration is necessary, as also are many other things; let the soul " believe in the light;" God will not neglect *His* work.

Two railway travellers were conversing on this subject. Said one:—

" I have the Book that makes known eternal life, but I cannot say that I *have* it. I want to *feel* that I have it."

It was replied: " When the clerk laid your ticket on the window-board this morning, did you say, ' I must first feel that I have this ticket before I take it?' Or did you first take it, and then feel that you had it?"

Many are led by feeling instead of faith. The " feeling " follows: it does not precede. Even then its distinctness, its precise nature, and the rapidity of its following, can be indicated by no rule. Nor was it designed that it should be subject to a ceaseless and morbid self-examination. The soul's " look " must be an out-look,

not a look within; to Christ, not self. "Look
unto *Me*," not for a moment only, but ever.
The Christian's motto is, "Looking unto Jesus
the Author *and Finisher* of our faith."

> "My hope is built on nothing less
>   Than Jesus' blood and righteousness;
> I dare not trust the sweetest frame,
> But *wholly* lean on Jesus' name.
> On Christ, the solid Rock, I stand:
> All other hope is — sinking sand!"

"My father," said a young man, "was as good
a man as was in all the parish, but he could not
say he was saved; no, not even when dying.
At that solemn moment, he was anxious for
some token" —

"Token! What do you mean, pray?"

"Mean? Why I mean he expected, or wished
to see, or hear, or feel, *something* to assure him
that he was going to heaven. But he got nothing, — no token."

The very vagueness of such a hope, as shown
when brought to the light in words, betrays its
uncertainty and its utter lack of warrant. The
Scriptures speak with no such uncertain sound.

There is a token, but it is not in the human heart. It is in the word: "Behold the *blood* shall be to you for a token!" And there is no other.

"A wicked and adulterous generation seeketh after a sign; but there shall no sign be given it but the sign of the prophet Jonas. For as Jonas was three days and three nights in the whale's belly, so shall the Son of Man be three days and three nights in the heart of the earth."

The resurrection is the sign, following upon the crucifixion and burial, and indicating Christ's finished work. The blood is the token. The promise in the Gospel is the warrant. The soul that will rest here may do so without fear. There is no other testimony to be had. No inward work or feeling is of value as an evidence.

3. This is not a question of achievements, as some suppose. The right to wear the name Christian is not in suspense until the performance of Christian labors. The order in nature and in grace alike is: first, the life; then the name; and the labors in due time afterward.

Paul was a Christian when he entered Damascus, when he had as yet done nothing for his Lord. The jailer at Philippi was a Christian when he arose to be baptized; yet a few moments before he had been an impenitent and apparently a hardened sinner. He had indeed asked, in his ignorance, " What must I *do* to be saved ? " But, the answer omitting " doing " entirely, the word was, " *Believe* on the Lord Jesus Christ, and thou shalt be saved."

True, the Master has said : —

" Not every one that saith unto me ' Lord, Lord,' shall enter into the kingdom of heaven; but he that doeth the will of my Father which is in heaven."

But the same lips elsewhere add the interpretation : —

" And this *is* His will, that ye *believe* on Him whom He hath sent ! "

So far as *becoming* a Christian is concerned, it is quite true that : —

"Nothing, either great or small,
Remains for thee to do;
Jesus did it, did it all,
Long, long ago.

> " When He from His lofty throne
>   Stooped down to do and die,
> Every thing was fully done ;
>   ' 'Tis finished ! ' was His cry."

Wherefore, in order to become a Christian :

> " Cast your deadly doings down,
>   Down, all, at Jesus' feet ;
> Stand in Him, in Him alone,
>   All glorious and complete."

4. Some stand in doubt of themselves because they have failed to attain to their ideal. Such persons either misuse the true ideal, or they erect a false one.

The true ideal, and goal, of the Christian life is the perfect manhood exemplified in Christ : —

> " Till we all come, in the unity of the faith and of the knowledge of the Son of God, unto a perfect man, unto the measure of the stature of the fulness of Christ. . . . That we . . . may grow up into Him in all things."

No one has attained this perfection. It is our goal, not our beginning. Are there, then, no Christians? Preposterous!

The Christian life begins by birth, is feeble

at first, and advances by a slow process of growth, sometimes very irregularly. And this whole process is inner and invisible. It is not at any time susceptible of measurement by mortal man.

Moreover, there is no standard of measurement save Christ. Men erect standards, often from observation of some saintly lives; and herein men err. Such standards are unwarranted, and the measurements by which they are obtained cannot but be grossly inaccurate. The use of any such "standard" must produce mischief. Nothing may be allowed to take the eyes from the Master. The soul has enough to do in striving for growth in Him, up to His fulness; any withdrawal of the look and cessation of the effort, in order to a vain attempt to measure the distance travelled or to note the point attained, is but a sinful folly.

Any measurement of one's self by men, whether in respect of the "experience," the "stature" or the "conduct" in grace, is a blunder, resulting from disuse of the light and walking in darkness; and this is true whether the measurement be in the interests of self-conceit or of self-depreciation: " they, measuring themselves by themselves and comparing themselves among themselves, are not wise."

Many say they have such an exalted conception of what the Christian ought to be that they dare not call themselves Christians: they are "only trying to be" Christians. These are wiser than their Master. In truth, although no doubt unconsciously, they are too proud to be considered Christians at all until they can be such admirable Christians that observers shall brand them "superior" and "first-class." They are grossly in error. They stumble; and others fall over them.

The Scriptures speak only of "babes" in Christ, of "growth" in grace, and of "perfect manhood." Every one must begin as a "babe." It is inquired whether the reader have begun; not whether he have become so mature a Christian that he may trust somewhat in himself, for that may never be. Still, as ever, the Saviour asks, " Dost thou believe on the Son of God ? "

5. This is not a question of creeds, but of the person of Christ. Is there faith in Him?

Half-witted Tom sought admission to the church as a Christian. He was asked for a confession of his faith. His sole answer was the singing of a couplet which he had learned from a dying sailor: —

> " I 'm a poor sinner and nothing at all ;
> But Jesus Christ is my All in All."

He was refused admission and went away much grieved. Returning to renew his application, he uttered the same statement of his faith; and so eager did he seem and so evident did it become that he knew the meaning of the words he uttered, that he was at length received.

It was enough. No larger creed is necessary. It needs but that the soul relinquish all hope of safety save in Christ, and receive Him as its salvation. The sinner is brought face to face with the Saviour. There the two stand alone. The Master speaks. He seeks the sinner's trust, his confidence in His own person: "Dost thou believe on the Son of God?"

6. "But I must repent; I have not yet repented enough."

The twofold action contemplated in the Saviour's question is repentance and faith in one. The tangible feature of repentance is the act of *turning;* turning from wrong to right, from error to truth, from sin to salvation. All these ends meet in Christ: "He that hath the Son hath life." Turning from all else, "Dost thou believe on the Son of God?"

The soul is sick unto death. The disease is sin. — Christ is the Physician.

Man is justly condemned by the law, for sin. — "Christ hath redeemed us from the curse of the law, being made a curse for us."

The divine life has gone out of the soul because of sin. A new life must be imparted. — "He is our life."

The disciple is still frail; he sins still.— "If any man sin, we have an Advocate with the Father, Jesus Christ the righteous!"

We are under the sway of sin. — Christ is King. An old catechism wisely teaches that " Christ as our Redeemer executeth the office of a King by subduing us unto himself, by ruling and defending us, and by restraining and conquering all His and our enemies." He said: " Ye call me Master and Lord; and ye say well, for so I am."

Man is in darkness by reason of sin in darkness as to truth, duty and destiny. — Christ is " the light of men." Is all other guidance sacrificed and surrendered for the guidance of Christ, in all matters, whether of doctrine, of duty, or of hope?

In a word: so far as the soul has ascertained its needs, is Christ accepted as the full supply, the One " *mighty* to save," " able to save *to the uttermost* all that come unto God by Him?"

> " The whole world was lost in the darkness of sin:
> The Light of the world is Jesus.
> Like sunshine at noonday His glory shone in:
> The Light of the world is Jesus.
> Come to the Light: 'tis shining for thee.
> Sweetly the Light has dawned upon me,
> Once I was blind, but now I can see:
> The Light of the world is Jesus."

"Just as I am! without one plea
But that thy blood was shed for me,
And that thou bidst me come to thee,
　　O Lamb of God, I come.

"Just as I am! poor, wretched, blind!
Sight, riches, healing of the mind,
Yea all I need, in thee to find,
　　O Lamb of God, I come."

D

II.

LOCATING THE LIGHT.

"Thy word is a lamp unto my feet, and a light unto my path." — Ps. cxix. 105.

WHEN one has definitely ascertained that he is a Christian, he must needs begin to reckon himself one of that countless and varied host divinely termed "disciples," "believers," "saints," "children of light." Whatever is authoritatively said to these in general, is specifically addressed to him — whether it be promise, precept or reproof, permission or restraint, comfort or rebuke : it is his own.

Where shall this authoritative address be found?

Manifestly, the disciple must be directed by his Master. The thought is subject to His teaching, and the conduct subject to His will. The Christian's motto is, "Looking unto Jesus, the Author and Finisher of our faith." Christ completes what He undertakes. The soul is surrendered to His hands. He " is made unto us wisdom and righteousness and sanctification and redemption." He is *every thing* to the believer. He is his Prophet and his King, as fully and as necessarily as his Priest: the disciple must be subject to His constant guidance and His unremitting rule, as well as to the daily application of His sacrificial blood. For the terms are given: " Whosoever he be of you that forsaketh not all that he hath, cannot be my disciple." Christ is the Guide: " I am the light." " He that followeth me shall not walk in darkness, but shall have the light of life."

But where is this light? The voice that was heard in Galilee is not heard among us now. Jesus is seized from our sight. Whither shall we look for guidance?

There is something significant in the double coincidence which assigns the same names to Jesus the Person, and the Book, the Bible. He was known as " the Word," " the Word of

God." On the eve of His departure, in His intercessory prayer, He took up this name and left it behind attached to the Scriptures. He prayed, "Sanctify them through thy truth; thy word is truth."

He was also self-styled " the light," and this name too has been attached to the Bible : " Thy word is a lamp unto my feet, and a light unto my path."

There these names still cling ; and justly, for the Bible is to us what Jesus was to the first disciples — the revealer of God's thought. Christ is the revelation of God : the Bible is the revelation of Christ, and *thereby* the revelation of God. " The Bible is neither a code of morals nor a system of doctrine, but the revelation of a Person." It is the expression, in writing, of the truths and precepts which Jesus illustrated in His life, and spake with His lips. It is Christ reduced to rule and promise in human language. His explicit command and statement are : " Search the Scriptures : . . . these are they which testify of me."

Christ quotes from the Old Testament, and appropriates it as His own. His own words and the inspired record of His deeds, form the beginning and basis of the New Testament; and on that basis the rest of it was built, at His command, and under the promised direction of the Holy Ghost. The whole Book is animated by His Spirit. JESUS is the golden thread running through the sixty-six fragments and uniting them in one living structure. The one Christ, in various forms of revelation, appears throughout. The type and the prophecy, the song and the sacrifice, the ritual and the history of the Old Testament, speak of Christ and for Christ as certainly, as constantly and as accurately, if not as completely, as do the sermons, the biographies and the epistles of the New. Christ built the Book. He speaks through it. It is His representative as the light of men. To this book, as to Him, the disciple must come for cheer and comfort, for doctrine and reproof — for the guidance of all thought and action.

True, Christians also are declared to be

"lights in the world," and in the aggregate, as
the church, "the light of the world." This,
however, is in subordination to the Scriptures.
The Word is the storehouse of instruction, the
authoritative revelation, the immediate and dis-
tinctive representative of Jesus as the light of
men: "To the law and to the testimony; if
any man speak not according to this Word, it
is because there is no light in them." No lesser
luminary may be ignored, but it may not replace
the greater, or divide its dignity. He who
travels in utter darkness on an unknown and
dangerous way, relies *for guidance* on the lamp
he carries, though he find use also for the flickering fires by the roadside. The Bible is the
guiding light. It has been so furnished with
latent material for illumination, that its capabilities cannot be overmatched by any emergency
or exhausted by any length of use: "All Scripture is given by inspiration of God, and is profitable for doctrine, for reproof, for correction, for
instruction in righteousness; that the man of
God may be perfect, *thoroughly furnished* unto

all good works." Small as the volume is to human sight and touch, it yet is so condensed, so wisely free from useless elements, and so divinely preshaped to the individual needs of believers severally, as to comprise all that any Christian need be told in order to the full direction of his thought and conduct.

Moreover, this is no mere book. The eye does not fall upon mere dead print. The living Voice still echoes in these chambers. The promise is, "Lo I am with you alway." Christ's Spirit still lingers in these sacred pages. The Book is inspired — it breathes!

It is true that a certain life and power are imparted also to the books of men — something of thought lies behind the dead letter; but the degree of difference between these and the Book of God, is so great as to become a bridgeless gulf: it is infinite. It is like the difference between the ordinary quantities of mathematics, and the "infinite quantity" whose powers are beyond the range of calculation; between the ordinary facts of science, and the realm of fact

termed "the unknowable;" between the finite
and circumscribed life of man, and the being of
Him who is " from everlasting to everlasting — "
man has a certain " life," but God is *life*.   The
so-called "inspiration" of human writings is
derived, circumscribed and adulterated, so that
they are utterly devoid of fitness *for guidance*
save, at second-hand, as reflecting the thought
of God.   The inspiration of the Bible, on the
other hand, is such as to make it the constant channel for the immediate and exact
conveyance of God's thought to every man
to whom it is sent, for every emergency when he
may use it, and up to the point of time when
it may be the Giver's pleasure to lay it aside.

This Book is so fashioned that peculiar messages, suited to his needs, are hidden in the let-
tered shell for each believer, which another may
not find there, and which he finds only as the
needs arise.   There is a personal and present
communion between the soul and the Master
through these records: " God . . . hath spoken
unto us by His Son," and still speaks. " He [the

Holy Spirit] shall receive of mine and show it
unto you " — progressively, as occasion requires
and application is made. The same short passage holds concealed a myriad messages for the
myriad wants of myriad men, prepared *not* " on
general principles," but on definite foreknowl-
edge of the personal needs of each at every
moment of time.

Thus the Scriptures become to the believer
the living voice of God, the voice of Jesus the
God-revealer, addressing *him* in tender accents
which the ear may almost catch, and with a
specific and exact adaptation of meaning and of
manner which attest the directness and person-
ality of the address. To him who will receive
the Book as it is, as " the revelation of the Person, Christ Jesus," addressed to him, who will
surrender himself to its guidance, will bathe
himself in its atmosphere and saturate his
thought with its expressions, and will resort to
it both habitually and in emergency, it will
prove itself, through the animating Spirit, at
least as adequate a light as Jesus was to the first

3*

disciples.* It was designed to be nothing less than this.

It has so proved itself already, in the experience of every Christian. The soul has found its living Saviour through His speech in the words of Scripture. He is found nowhere else. Some one text, at least, was made to breathe, to utter its voice, to give the conviction of a Saviour speaking through it in personal and direct address. Else had not the soul believed.

All that is now needed is to enlarge the scope. The same Jesus speaks throughout. The whole matter of salvation, including the guidance of all thought and action, is purely a personal affair between the soul and Christ; at no point an affair of creeds, churches, Christian opinion, or general rules of human devising. And in His conduct of the soul forward step by step, Christ

* *See* John xvi. 7: "It is expedient for you that I go away," &c. Christ indicates that the teaching of the Holy Ghost, being spiritual and unhampered by the claims of the flesh, is more effective and comprehensive than His own could be. Our privileges exceed those enjoyed by His nearest personal friends!

employs His whole word as a vehicle of address, address fresh, direct and apt: "*All* Scripture is . . . profitable," &c.

Did the believer find Christ elsewhere? He heard Him speaking through these records, and here only in the last analysis: for His voice — the shining of His light — through Christians, to which some give attention, is due to *their* having heard Him here; they are "lights in the world" only as they follow Him, only as they receive Him to their hearts and exhibit Him in their lives.

Accordingly, the dilemma is: the whole Bible, or no Christ; a dilemma from which there is no escape; for all the authority He claimed for himself as Teacher, He claims for this Book as used by His Spirit.

It would therefore be to the last degree irrational, for the Christian at least, to refuse or to disuse the Bible as the rule of his life; or to listen in preference to any other voice, touching any matter whatever of either faith or conduct.

Some seem still to doubt the practical value
of the written Word for guidance in the minutiæ of life.   What then?

1. The Saviour bids us resort to it : " *Search* ·
the Scriptures ; . . . these are they which testify of me."   His word by the mouth of David
is, " Thy word is a lamp *unto my feet*, and a
light unto my path."   " Wherewithal shall a
young man cleanse his *way?* by taking heed
thereto according to thy word."   And everywhere the impression is distinctly conveyed that
Christians require and may obtain constant and
most minute direction through the Bible.

2. The fundamental law of life is, " Whether
therefore ye eat, or drink, or whatever ye do,
do all to the glory of God."   This law certainly
requires frequent contact with " the mind of
Christ " as He presents it in His word.   How
else can the conduct be regulated by a rule so
sweeping, and so foreign to the common
thought?   How else can true motive be cultivated and maintained?   We have been so used
to act from other motives than love to the

Redeemer; we are so tempted by common and seemingly harmless custom to act still upon other principles and to other ends than the glory of God; that there needs to be a constant struggle for possession of the Bible-spirit and for familiarity with Bible-precept; else we shall waste our years in hopeless straying!

3. We are weak. The treasures of grace which we enjoy are kept in " earthen vessels." It is easy for us to do wrong, and at the same time persuade ourselves that we do right. There must be constant " correction;" and " All Scripture is profitable . . . for correction."

4. The Bible is not on so lofty a plane, nor are its pages so filled with other things, as to separate it from the petty needs of our daily life. It was meant to be the guide, not only to our more elevated thoughts, but also to our most unimportant acts. And as befits a book designed for common use, by common people and in common affairs, its style is simple, its address is direct, its precepts abound, and it

presents a vast number of vivid and pertinent illustrations of the method of right conduct.

The Christian who places the Bible afar off, and considers his daily thought and behavior outside of or beneath its directions, misses the use of the vast wealth of provision which it contains. The bulk of the Book seems to him but an arid desert. Oases are few. He finds refreshment in but a promise here and a precept there. The rest is as barren and dry as Sahara. How many Christians speak of the Bible in just such terms! Their seeming poverty is the result of their own blunder. It is folly to squander resources so rich, so needful, and so apt.

The book of Proverbs may furnish an illustration. Would that our young men, especially our Christian business-men, were saturated with its thought! It is rich in practical wisdom for the minute affairs of common life. It abounds in apt and pointed suggestions and pungent warnings, concerning our companionships, our personal habits, our employments, our management of finance, our speech, the government of tongue and temper, and many other such things which daily perplex the earnest soul, and daily occasion harm to the thoughtless and the misguided. The minuteness, the precision, the comprehensiveness, the pungent *power* of these directions, are a never-ceasing marvel. And they come to the thoughtful Christian as the expression of his Master's present thought for his guidance ; so that he knows them to be correct, in the highest sense of the term.

In precepts of this sort, the Scriptures are rich throughout. The large room given to them in the book of Proverbs, merely suggests and illustrates one of the features of the entire Word.* ·

---

* Here is brought to view one beauty of this marvellous Production which few seem to have observed : *Every fragment of the Bible has its specialty, and that specialty marks a distinct feature of the entire Book, — a separate thread running through the whole volume.* By way of further instances, consider : *Genesis*, the book of beginnings, suggesting that the Bible reveals only the beginning of God's thought; rich as the revelation is, it affords a mere foretaste of our heavenly study and delight. *Exodus*, recording the " going out" of God's people *because of* their redemption by Blood : this thread runs through. *The*

Yet even here "the Bible is not a code of morals, ... but the revelation of a Person;" whence these precepts become the most binding species of law, — to him who owns that Person as his Lord and Master.

Added to this, we have biography, affording varied and vivid illustrations, not so much of virtue and vice in general, as of many definite excellences and faults of conduct in particular, and of their antecedents in correct or erroneous thought, and in correct or defective training and associations. The records concerning Noah, Abraham, Isaac, Jacob, Jephthah, Peter, Joseph, Solomon, Jonah, and Lot, respectively, furnish needed and forcible warning against drunkenness, falsehood, rashness in making vows or promises, unwise parental partialities, false self-reliance, imprudence of speech, irreligious do-

---

Gospels, biographies of Christ: the whole Bible speaks of Him. *The Epistles*, addressed to the several churches: the Bible is handed down to and brought out before men by and through the churches. *The Revelation*, a prophecy; the entire Bible, from Genesis iii. 15, is an index finger pointing forward to Christ's Second Coming and the glory that shall then be revealed.

mestic alliances, the shirking of unwelcome duty, and the neglect of religious associations in seeking a new home. Other such records expose other common errors of conduct, in their seeds, their nature, and their mischievous results. While, on the other hand, there is in these biographies a vivid and pleasing exhibition of such small virtues as thoughtfulness and cheerfulness, hospitality, persistence in the right, discreet management of business, &c.

These biographical records, although packed with a marvellous compression, nevertheless touch our common thought and conduct, our common perplexities and desires, at nearly every point, and with an almost electric power to win to the right and to affright from the wrong. In this, as in every other feature, the Bible is eminently, divinely practical. And here, as elsewhere, it is " the revelation of a Person," of Jesus in His brief, varied, and pointed exhibition of good and evil, of truth and error, of happiness and misery, and of the line of sequence from little things to great results. That is : we have here His present thought for His disciples, severally. *This* is " the best modern thought " !

Further : to give room for the independent growth of the individual judgment, — which the Bible everywhere seeks to stimulate, not to repress, — and to provide for possible questions of creed and duty not otherwise met, certain keynotes are struck for us here and there, certain ruling principles are given,* whose application to minutiæ men are to work out for themselves. These are the revelation of Jesus in His *lines* of thought. By the vigorous use of these principles alone, a discreet man might regulate all his study of truth and all the affairs of his life, large and trifling alike, with but few mistakes.

The Scriptures fully justify the names they bear, " the Word of God," " the Light," as the representative, and the constant, sufficient, and living utterance of Him who only is the Light of life and the Lawgiver of His people. This

---

* *See* Part Third, section iv., of this volume ; " The Laws of Light."

Book is fitly and necessarily made the rule by which the thought and the demeanor of Christians are to be entirely regulated.

This is insisted upon because it is fundamental. "If the foundations be destroyed, what can the righteous do?" This foundation has not been built upon by the masses; yet its use is essential to the best appeal and counsel, to the best Christian living, and to all steadiness of advance.

Notwithstanding this, the minds of many are turned in other directions. Some are turned to the traditions of the churches, some to factitious rules framed by men and often unwarranted by the Word, and some to common custom. We hear much of "what men say," of "what is considered right," of "the custom among our people," and of "the rules of the church" and "living up to them;" although, rightly, few churches have many "rules" for the direction of personal conduct.

No church may justly come between the soul and the Saviour, either when as a sinner he seeks salvation, or when as a saint he desires guidance. The church may only point to the Saviour as revealed in the Word, and this she should ever do. The Bible furnishes our only and a sufficient rule. Churches make mistakes. Public opinion, even the general opinion of Christians, often errs. The conscience of the believer is not bound. Even when the interests of Zion require of him deference to a rule or a custom for which he fails on search to find Scriptural warrant, this is only through the application of the Biblical law, "If meat make my brother to offend," &c. Thus to the last he bows to Christ alone, and acts only on Scriptural direction.

The Christian may not delegate to any body of men, or to any code of custom, the responsibility of forming his creed, of deciding questions of duty, or of furnishing him with habits of life. Thought, unduly pressed by the needs of a time, may crystallize into rules which will inevitably outlive their usefulness; and the conditions of one epoch may favor a license which sterner days had justly forbidden, and which may as justly be revoked upon their return. For all this variety of need, provision is made by the fulness and adaptability of Biblical suggestion ; and they err, to their own and others' hurt, who permit commentaries, books of discipline, the voice of the people, or any thing else, to take the place of the one sacred Book which was explicitly and laboriously prepared "to guide our way." Creeds, commentaries, books of discipline, have their places, important places ; but *this* place belongs to the Scriptures alone.

Some are infected with the insane notion that submission to the guidance of the Bible, even though this be but the personal and immediate guidance of Christ *through* the Bible, is an abnegation of the right of free thought. On the contrary, it is one of the fruits of free thought. To deny one's self its use is to invade his prerogative, not to strengthen it. Only the Christian who is thorough-going in his adhesion to the Scriptures can be a free-thinker ; he " walks in the light," and is certain that his decisions are correct and his conclusions just. Can men offer something better than this? Impossible! This is the very acme of privilege, of accuracy, of freedom.

He who robs his reason of those aids to information which the Christian has, — the teaching of the Spirit, the use of the Bible *as* Christ's infallible Word, and the enlightenment afforded by prayer, — and who binds his judgment to decision upon the wofully inadequate information that remains, instead of being a freethinker, is the slave of ignorance and prejudice. His judgments cannot fail to be crude, and usually false.

The Christian, on the other hand, is one who has endowed his judgment with its richest furniture of evidence and light. He permits himself to use, as being infallibly true and pertinent, the statements of God's word ; for, on principles which he cannot possibly reject, and by a short and simple process of reasoning, he has ascertained that those statements are valid, are the utterances of God Himself; and he would now feel impoverished if deprived of their use. He has also learned to employ prayer, and to await the matchless teaching of the Spirit. Thus he has placed himself directly under the beams of the Sun of Righteousness, thereby achieving a position in which he can make practical use of God's good gift to man, — an enfranchised private judgment.

To receive a certainty as truth is no invasion of intellectual freedom. One cannot help receiving it, and he who is sincere in his search for truth is glad to come upon the certainty. Simply this is what the Christian does. Moreover, he does this rationally, not blindly. He begins by following Jesus, it being utterly irrational to reject *His* claims, however startling they may be. Then, walking in this Light, he is inevitably conducted to the assurance that Scripture is the "light unto our path" provided by the Master. Then follows the walk in *that* light, as adequate, and as representing Jesus. Now walking in Light is the only freedom possible.

The Christian has here a heritage which should not be lightly sacrificed, nor its fruits refused or squandered. The vast benefits in the believer's reach by the faithful use of the Bible as his constant guide should be so prized, so eagerly sought, so firmly held, as to crown his days with light and gladness, and his whole life with its highest success.

> " 'Tis Revelation satisfies all doubt,
> Explains all mysteries, — except its own, —
> And so illuminates the path of life
> That fools discover it and stray no more."

PART SECOND.

MISTAKING DARKNESS FOR LIGHT.

(WORLDLINESS.)

"My kingdom is not of this world."—JOHN xviii. 36.

4

I. Stumbling.

II. Falling.

III. Maimed.

IV. Reproved and Recalled.

"Woe unto them that call evil good, and good evil; that put darkness for light, and light for darkness; that put bitter for sweet, and sweet for bitter." — Isa. v. 20.

I.

STUMBLING.

"If a man walk in the night, he stumbleth; because there is no light in *him!*" JOHN xi. 10.

THERE is an ellipsis in this utterance. As it stands, the emphasis is on the words "stumbleth" and "him;" — "If a man walk in the night, he stumbleth; because," it being night, there is no Light to guide him; and "there is no light *in him*," even for this emergency.

The underlying thought is patent and pertinent, — *Men should not walk in the night.* The impenitent do so of necessity, as such, and so long as they remain impenitent: they are children of the Night. But if Christians "walk in the night," they make an unnecessary sacrifice of prestige and privilege. Are they not "children of the Day"? Why should they lower themselves to the level of the "children of darkness"? Doing so, they become like them, —

that is, worldlings. They are guilty of worldliness, — *worldlikeness.*

And this is Worldliness, of which we hear so much.

"To sleep," to "walk in darkness," to "have fellowship with the unfruitful works of darkness," and to be "conformed to this world," are figurative expressions common in the Scriptures, and almost, if not quite, interchangeable. They all characterize worldliness.

This sin, then, lies in closing the eyes to the Light, in walking as men walk, and thinking as men think, paying little regard to any thing higher than public opinion and civil law. It is regulating the creed and life by other guidance than that of Christ. It has its origin in the neglect of close, constant, and vital consultation with the Master through His Word, and in the substitution of consultation with one's self and with' the opinions and customs of men.

Many are guilty of worldliness who are loud in its denunciation. They are sincere, but they are mistaken.

They are mistaken in supposing that worldliness lies only in matters of conduct, and chiefly in certain notable overt acts. They think, perhaps, that because they shun the dance, the theatre, and the company of the profane, because their conduct is set off from that of the impenitent by a certain religious air and a certain self-restraint, therefore *they* are not worldlings! The sin has a deeper root and a wider range than these suppose.

The slightest act performed without, or contrary to, the guidance of the Word; the slightest failure to do what the Word requires; even the slightest thought indulged, or decision as to truth reached, except by this guidance, — is a stumble in the dark, a piece of worldliness. Every Christian is guilty of this sin; is guilty as often and so far as he fails to realize in thought and behavior, the full practical value of the law, " Thy word is a lamp unto my feet, and a light unto my path."

The fallacy which makes religion a matter of external forms is subtle, widespread, and varied in its manifestations. It enters the realms of creed and conduct as well as the realm of public worship. There is as much formalism of Christian life as of Christian worship; and the former is even more to be deprecated than the latter. It were better to have the life right, even if it seem to express itself in worship somewhat stiffly, than to have but the appearance of life, and to have that appearance dressed in stiff and misleading travesty of Christian manners. "Man looketh on the outward appearance, but the Lord looketh on the heart." Wherefore "keep thy heart with all diligence, for out of it are the issues of life."

Undue stress should not be laid upon mere matters of dress, speech, and behavior. The great evils of worldliness are not here. And especially is it mischievous to indulge — as so many do — a worldly pride, upon account of the denial of certain worldly amusements and ambitions.

This tendency to emphasize appearances has led to many distortions of Christianity. The philosophy which makes, or which seems to make, godliness consist of words and acts alone, or chiefly; which censures rational enjoyment and cheerful demeanor; which pharisaically demands that Christians conform to a factitious line of conduct which their fellow-Christians have drawn, — is so grievous a distortion of Christianity as to amount to a grotesque travesty. The worst misrepresentations of which a hostile infidelity is guilty could not be more false than this, and they work less harm.

Stumbling does not proceed from inability to see at once all that the Light discloses. The eyes of the young are unused to the light; but their feet are kept.

The young Christian does not take in at a glance all the steeps he must attempt, and all the pitfalls he must avoid. He has yet much to learn. His earthly guides may seek to lay upon him commands which he has not had opportunity to receive direct from the Master. Until the opportunity be had, he does not sin by refusing or delaying obedience. For example: one may become a Christian without having first learned *upon authority,* that it is the Christian's first great duty to confess his Lord by achieving a church-membership; or that it is his duty to read his Bible daily, to lead others in vocal prayer upon occasion, to maintain the worship of God in the family, to give money for the support of the church and for the cause of missions, to render the aid of personal exertion to the work of evangelism. Not having learned, if he go forward in these things upon mere human pressure or mere blind impulse, he acts without sufficient warrant; he advances farther than he has learned the way.

Many Christians stumble so, forced ahead, perhaps, by too eager Christian friends and teachers. They are impelled further than the path is made plain before them, and so beyond the strength and wisdom given them. As a consequence, they break down. They rush ahead too hastily, stumble, and fall. — We have had too many Arthur Bonnicastles. — And it is inevitable that their fall should so astound them — inasmuch as they thought they were but doing God service — as to give their Christian life a shock: it becomes dwarfed; growth is checked for a long time to come.

When, on the other hand, the opportunity to learn is neglected, the stumbling is as certain to follow as before. To delay the act of entering the church, or any thing else that is enjoined, longer than is absolutely necessary to the ascertainment of the duty as duty, is sin. It is to link one's self with the world unduly. The eyes being open to the Light, they should use it vigilantly in discerning the path; and action should follow promptly, at whatever cost.

All this is as true when applied to the thought as when it directly affects the conduct. "The truth" is a possession "more precious than rubies."

> "Buy the truth
> And sell it not."
> "Get wisdom,
> Get understanding."

For the thought will influence the behavior: —

4* F

" Receive my words . . .
   Then shalt thou understand the fear of the Lord,
   And find the knowledge of our God, . . .
   That thou mayst walk in the way of good men,
   And keep the paths of the righteous."
" Happy is the man that findeth wisdom,
   And the man that getteth understanding.

   .   .   .   .

   Her ways are ways of pleasantness,
   And all her paths are peace."

The formation and the constant correction of opinion by the Word are duties which rest on every Christian from the first. Failure to discharge these duties will work harm. To omit independent study of the Scriptures, and to neglect the sermon or the private counsel which might stimulate and aid it, may be common, but it is mischievous. To frame a creed or any part of one, or to subscribe to one that others have framed, without having first drawn it from the Book of God's wisdom for one's self; to permit others or another — a church, a pastor, a newspaper, or a school of science — to shape one's thought: is to close the eyes to the Light, and so far to walk in darkness and stumble.

Because of the power of past habit and present associations, there is constant danger of this kind of mistake. It seems almost impossible *not* to shape the life upon the rules of society, not to do as men do, as respectable people do, or at best as older Christians do ; not to think as men think or as the church suggests. It is, after all, a marvel that all Christians are not thorough worldlings. That there is so much devotion as appears, much of it eager and sustained, is nothing less than a miracle. Only Omnipotent grace could have produced it.

There be many who " put darkness for light, and light for darkness." We are told of the light of reason, the inner light, the light of civilization, and many other supposed daymakers. There is always a strong and steady drift toward forming the opinions and framing the life under the guidance of these *ignes fatui*. Even good books, church-standards, and Christian customs may serve to mislead. . Any thing to form men's notions and to shape their conduct by another rule than God's rule.

Sometimes it is urged that the Bible was not

designed to guide our commoner thoughts and actions; sometimes, that its precepts were designed only for those to whom they first came. Any thing to displace or disparage the Light, and make room for false and inadequate substitutes.

Sometimes the substitute is science; social science, physiological science, the science of trade. Science may yield aid *so far as it is the legitimate product of the Scriptures;* further than that it must mislead: science has no light of its own.

Sometimes it is the reason. But the reason is of use only to receive, arrange, and digest information. The reason can give no information, has no light of its own.

There is nothing so good as to follow the Master: —

"If any man walk in the day he stumbleth not, because he seeth the Light of this world."

"He that followeth me shall not walk in darkness, but shall have the Light of life."

II.

FALLING.

"If the blind lead the blind, both shall fall into the ditch."
— MATT. xv. 14.

WHEN the Christian follows man rather than God, he is sure to fall. This false following is common, and the falls are frequent.

Some start wrong. Neglecting to discern or to obey the command which makes membership in the church a first and imperative duty, they remain, so far, "of the world ;" perhaps upon the plausible plea that "one may be as good a Christian out of the church as in it." So at the very outset the Scriptures are ignored as the guide of life.

The error brings a hurt. The Christian life in these people is dwarfed. They are exposed to much unnecessary temptation, and deprived of much needed support and stimulus. Some of the most efficient of the appointed means of

Christian culture are unused, and ere long neglect is apt to be put upon the others. So there grow up no rugged virtue, no burning zeal. There is rather decay. Even the hope of salvation is apt to dwindle and die out. Faith wanes. Charity pines. Sin finds an easy prey.

Years afterward, having been "recovered out of the snare" into which they had been "led captive," they may come forward to claim a place among Christians, as many such have done, with confession of the error committed in the first refusal or postponement. But the years past are beyond recall.

Mrs. K—— resided in the midst of the opportunities of the church. Her attendance was careless and fitful, yet she became a Christian. She chose to conceal her conversion. She learned from the Scriptures that the Christian should become a member of the church, but for reasons of her own she determined not to do so. After a time, she grew steadily less hopeful, and less faithful even in her home. She even ceased to attend divine service. When asked about becoming a child of God, her answers were so vague that the facts in her case were not discovered, and her manner was so curt as to repel further inquiry. Probably no one surmised the truth.

Thus passed eleven unprofitable and unsatisfactory years. Then Providence, ever co-operating with Grace, interposed to arouse her from lethargy. She was driven to her Bible. There she was forcibly reminded of her duty, and she saw her folly in neglecting it so long. She sought an interview with the pastor of a neighboring church. To him she confessed with sadness her neglect of duty. With tears she lamented the unhappy state of her household. She asked when she could be received to membership in the —— church, that she might " begin again," and thenceforth exert a healthier and more vigorous influence, in her home at least.

This case has many parallels.

Others so seek this membership as to vitiate its sacredness. They " join " because friends

wish them or tell them to do so, not because
Christ commands it. Thus the act falls short
of its hallowing influence, and becomes a semi-
hypocrisy. Hosts of our "ten millions of
communicants" do not know why they are
communicants, and realize but feebly the privi-
léges and responsibilities of their position;
and, having begun by doing as others do or
say, their whole life is at second hand.

Many determine what particular church to
enter, from purely human motives. They go
with their friends, or where social advantages
offer, or where financial obligations are easy,
or where the type of piety is not exacting or
stimulating, or where but little work will be
expected of them, or where membership may
prove profitable in a business way! This may
all be well, but these should not be the decisive
considerations. Divine guidance might lead
elsewhere, — where the Master needs His disciple. Duty may require the very choice that
is made, but it should be made *as* duty, not as
policy; else the association of Christians gained,

seen in the lurid glare of a false motive, will seem less than sacred, and must yield far less than it should of stimulus and growth. How many of our "ten millions" are indulging in the carnal luxury of a selfish church-membership!

The conduct of many in the church is regulated by mere worldly principles. They receive the teachings of the pulpit as correct, without bringing them to the Light for examination. Or if those teachings prove displeasing, they are rejected in the same arbitrary way.

Many seek and cherish petty place and power in the church.

It is sometimes sought to "manage the church on business principles," and those the "principles" of unsound business. Churches are built at greater expense than the needs and the circumstances of the people warrant, entailing wanton and baneful debt. The large congregation of the —— church in the city of O—— has only recently made a narrow escape from sale under the sheriff's hammer for a debt

of $90,000. Its cost was $175,000. Energies
and efforts are diverted from legitimate channels for concentration on this matter of the
debt, and must be for years to come. Meanwhile, perhaps the church may do some service
for the Master — incidentally!

It is sought to "advertise" churches by
conducting the worship, notably the service of
song, in such form as will captivate the popular
ear, rather than wing the devotion or minister
to the needs of the Christian heart. The pulpit
is sometimes subjected to the same misrule.
Money is raised "for the church" by questionable means. Churches are made to seem rivals.
Proselytism creeps in. It is sought to report a
large roll and a long list of charitable gifts,
through sheer pride.

At times, even the ministry are enveloped in
the cloud to a painful extent. The service of
Christ is made subordinate to ambition, to love
of lucre or of ease, to rancor and hate. The
spirit of folly steals into church-meetings, both
the assemblies of the local society and the

larger denominational gatherings. Discipline is shirked, "for fear — !" Creeds are pruned or hidden from sight, merely to please men. In fine, the Bible would sometimes seem to have entirely lost its place as the guide.

So the energies of many are wasted on worldly and unfruitful trifles, or in seeking good ends vainly by false methods. The spirit of piety shrivels. Money is squandered or withheld. Prayer withers into formality, or ceases. And Christians and churches who should walk in the Light, holding up their own feeble, imparted lights for the guidance of men, themselves mistake darkness for light, stumble, — and fall !

The conduct of many Christians in the home is any thing but becoming to the children of Light. God is not recognized as God of the house. Family prayer and counsel are neglected, "because I can't;" and this is the cant which is doing more harm than that other sort at which men so fiercely shriek. Parental responsibility is evaded, and opportunity neglected. The Word is not taught. The law of God is not *enforced* in the family as He requires. Cheerfulness, forbearance, self-restraint, self-denials, are not practised, *especially by Christian husbands and fathers!* And so the home, which should have been made a power for righteousness, operating constantly on all its inmates transient and permanent, and sending out its rays of light and healing far and wide, by every visit and by every guest, becomes — not a nonentity in the work of grace, but — a stumbling-block in the path of its advance : " If the light that is in thee be darkness, how great is that darkness ! "

The business life of many Christians is regulated entirely by the rules of man, whereas it should be regulated solely by the law of God. Tricks of trade are sometimes indulged. There is too great eagerness to be rich. Too great risks are undertaken. Excitement is too much cultivated. Too many debts are incurred. Unnecessary complications are permitted, and even courted. The man of business wearies himself unduly each day, and goes almost to the point of exhaustion, or even prostration, before Saturday night closes in; so that he cheats his family, his own soul, and the church out of their rightful claim upon his evenings and his Sabbaths.

At times, none too rare, there follow speculation, false entries, fraud, bribery; and how much more each reader of the daily newspaper knows only too well.

Society imposes its rules; and many Christians accept them without a question, without a thought of testing them by the Word. Evil companionships are tolerated. Social lines drawn by the world are permitted to govern the Christian, although they bring some associations which should be excluded, and exclude some which should be sought; and although they impose some obligations, taxing time and means, which should be disowned, and disown others which should be imposed and discharged.

Few of the current social habits, or even amusements, are wrong *per se;* but the tendency of many of them is evil, and indulgence in them is seen to work harm with a frequency that is unpleasantly suggestive.

Moreover, Society ignores duties which Christ commands ; for example, the kind of gathering to which " the poor, the maimed, the halt, the blind " are called. The fashionable world is content to relegate all such work to " those queer people who are *so* absurd ! " or to some association for newsboys and boot-blacks.

Society puts " the successful man " above the man of honor and honesty ; limits one's duties to one's own "set ; " and is apt to belittle the claims of the needy and the ignorant, especially those beyond the range of its immediate vision : " the world " does not affect the cause of Foreign Missions !

In all these things, Christians often drift with the current when they should ascertain *duty*, stem the tide if necessary, and do right at all hazards. It is not meant that Society should be unnecessarily assailed, nor yet that its just claims should be offensively disregarded. On

the contrary, deference should be shown whenever — as is usually the case, perhaps — those
claims are just. But the Christian should ever
have a higher law and walk by it, even in his
deference to human requirements and his consideration for others' tastes.

The latest, and in some respects the most
damaging species of worldliness is of quite another kind. It is exhibited in a worldly criticism of the Light itself, a *quasi* air of superiority
to the Bible. Some portions of it are neglected,
then contemned. Some of its doctrines and
precepts are disowned. Its ordinances, especially the Sabbath and the Church, are mutilated
by hands profane. The loosest rationalistic
criticism is permitted (most *ir*rationally) to
shave off here and to puncture there, till but a
remnant of the Book is left — for the critic!
and even that remnant is shorn of moral power,
is stripped of its just authority as a guide to
faith and morals.

The reaction from this folly to looseness of
life, is natural and inevitable. The critic him-

self may maintain his former habits of integrity, —scarcely the habits of devoted piety, — but the folly is transmitted to those who have not been so staunchly built or so well grounded. Thus families, churches, and communities deteriorate in a generation or two, until open immorality sets in and makes the mischief evident to all.

" If the blind lead the blind, both shall fall into the ditch ! "

III.

MAIMED.

"They have erred from the faith, and pierced themselves through with many sorrows." — 1 Tim. vi. 10.

IT is impossible to make a single misstep without injury. It may be the crushing of gems or flowers; it may be the spraining of the misplaced foot; it may seem simply delay in one's progress: harm of some sort is certain to follow the mistake.

" The wages of sin is death." The slightest sin tends to disintegration and decay; some valuable interest is invariably injured or destroyed.

Some forms of worldliness wear the garb of innocence. " An innocent pleasure," " an innocent ambition," are names which often serve to entice the unwary. The innocence is only apparent. Behind it lurks some subtle, unsuspected poison. Whenever the enticement

G

prevails, some one suffers, "pierced through with many sorrows."

The churches suffer. The absence of converted men from their places among the members, serves to weaken and dishearten those who are bearing the burdens and doing the work. The church is doubly weakened: in a partisan canvass every vote counts two.

A vacant church in the goodly town of H——, once reported to a visiting clergyman a roll of but twenty members, and greeted him on the Sabbath with an audience of ten persons. He was informed that the town was suffering immeasurably from infidelity, intemperance, feebleness of social life, duplicity in trade, a general want of public spirit, and all the earlier symptoms of decay. There were several other churches, each with about the same strength. All the active Christians in the community were disheartened, and the corporate life of the several Christian bodies was feeble, — so feeble that even their weakness could not bring them to unite in any good work. Some years after-

ward, a season of evangelistic labor disclosed
at least one of the sources of this decay : there
were found to be not far from one hundred
Christians in the community, — including many
men and women of culture, means, and social
influence, — entirely disconnected from the
churches, many of them being generally reckoned mere moralists, if not sceptics. They had
shrunk from assuming the responsibilities of
membership ; * and, as a consequence, the cause
of righteousness had nearly lost its foothold !
It is said that many of these persons afterward
took their places in the churches, but the evil
wrought could not be undone.

The presence of worldlings in the church is
an evil only less grave. The influence they
yield is that of an iceberg which some warm
wind has torn loose from its Arctic moorings
and driven into milder seas, into whose waters
it brings a deadly chill. Contact and contagion

* It must have been that the churches also had neglected
their duties. Such a state of affairs is altogether anomalous.
On any other supposition, it would seem impossible.

follow. Ardor is dampened. Piety wanes. Warmth oozes away. The whole atmosphere of the church becomes chilled and mouldy. Worldly fashion creeps in, becomes law. The church grows proud of its respectability, its wealth, its culture, its large and fashionable audiences, its influence in the community; and this pride is fed by a transition to a gaudy and costly church-building, a sensational pulpit, and an operatic service of song.

Then come scandals. A prominent member is convicted of fraud. One of the officers is found to have indulged, habitually and systematically for half a score of years, in glaring social crime. The pastor himself becomes involved in the toils and is disgraced. The very foundations of the church are shaken. People are horrified at the revelations made, and shun its doors. Its name becomes a by-word. Before lost prestige be restored, there must be a tedious gap, to be filled by the painful work of discipline and a prolonged humiliation before God.

This progressive statement may seem unwar-

ranted. Not so : it might not unfairly serve
as an approximately accurate history in outline
of the —— church in the city of ——, for a
period of fifteen years within the memory of
living men; an extreme case no doubt, yet the
case of a church that had had unsurpassed
antecedents and unusual advantages.

Worldliness in a milder form prevailed in the
church in the little village of S——. After
some years of comparative indifference, the
newspaper and " the claims of the time " were
allowed to a great extent to displace the claims
of the Bible and the church. As time passed,
the reading of the Scriptures · became widely
ignored, family religion declined, and preaching
almost ceased. It was not long until the social
life of the community was almost hopelessly
shattered by alienations ; until many other petty
evils crept in ; and until infidelity attained such
strength that its adherents and assemblages
quite overshadowed those of the church. The
Cross became an object of contumely, and in
some cases the subject of ridicule, among the

greater number of the more intelligent people of the town.

It is said that all this was afterward changed; the conditions were quite reversed. But these wasted years can never be recalled, nor the mischief wrought, erased.

Another community, within the limited reach of the same observer, presents a record very similar in the general features named. It is not unlikely that a score of illustrations of a like nature might be found in our own land alone.

The *misguided soul* also suffers.

The inner life of the Christian is a sensitive thing. As a breath for a time bedims the polished mirror; as the careless touch of its surface by so much as a needle-point defaces it: so the life of the soul is darkened and marred by every sin. Worldliness, being usually habitual and constant, produces a prolonged dimness and a deep defacement. The joys depart. Peace yields to unrest. The stimulus, the thrill, the throb of a generous life, wear away and return no more; supineness supplants zeal;

murmurings against other Christians often displace commendations of them; and gloomy doubt, or the love of unworthy things, occupies the room once held by the delights of ardent and successful service.

Worse things follow. The habit of neglecting or rejecting the guidance of the Scriptures becomes fixed, and the soul plunges deeper into the night, continually making fresh blunders and incurring fresh disasters.

It is of the nature of worldliness to grow. It pervades the soul gradually, and enfolds it slowly and steadily. It is impossible to set a limit to the process, save by revolutionizing the conduct and "steering by a new pole-star." Mere good intention will not prevent accession to the distress. No one can foresee into what blunders of life, what disappointments of pleasing expectation, what immoralities and even disgrace, the Christian may fall who walks otherwise than with a constant following of his Guide.

The wrecks of once promising lives; the

ruins of once honorable professions, of fair names and joyful hearts, — are found all over the land, in almost every city, village and rural community where faithful men seek the wayward and the wandering. The majority of these devastated lives are never rehabilitated ; the soul usually passes away in death from beneath the smothering fragments of the ruin, and weeping Christian friends are left to commit it, in awful doubt of its destiny, into the hands of Him who knoweth the secrets of all hearts.

He who, intoxicated with self-confidence, hoots at the possibility of such a fall in his case, is usually on the very brink of shame ; — like Simon Peter when, in the face of the Master's warning, he boasted, " Though all men should be offended because of thee, yet will not I." That night he fell! "Let him that thinketh he standeth take heed lest he fall." Only he who steps back aghast upon the opening of such a chasm at his feet, recognizing his danger, is likely to escape falling headlong into it.

The approaches of sin are sometimes gradual, like the steady tread of civilization across this continent, occupying as it goes, and driving all hostile life before it, step by step. In such cases, after a time, the soul is usually pressed further and further into the night; and it submits to each new pressure, to almost any limit, rather than endure the terrible wrench of tearing loose and turning back, and the terrific and protracted conflict necessary to regain its position and reconquer its heritage.

Sometimes in one unwatchful moment, akin to the hour of sleep in Gethsemane, a surprising and peculiarly apt temptation seizes the soul, and at once hurls it down from the heights to an infamous depth.

A—— and G—— were the sons of American clergymen of devoted piety and of good report. Both were undoubted Christians. Each, in his turn, leaning upon self instead of Christ, confident of the power of habit and the guidance of " the inner light," grew careless of search for God's thought through His Word, and of tem-

5*

pering the spirit and conduct by fresh divine
influence and direction. In the one case, in
early youth a grave and surprising temptation
overcame all the habits and the resolves of
piety at one blow, and the young man of many
hopes and of much self-confidence fell into the
grossest sin. He remained its slave for ten
years. In the other case, the declension was
gradual; each step seemed slight by the time
it was reached; it required but a series of
temptations little out of the ordinary line to
break down the barriers of virtue one by one,
and to swamp in the basest vice a life that had
for years seemed fair and full of promise, and
which had been so deemed by its possessor.
He, too, remained in bondage for years. What
these two men endured during their slavery,
what conscience thrusts, what unmitigated
shame; and what an abhorrence of self grew
up in them, — no mortal can tell. Their own
narrations were painfully suggestive, but evidently the half was not told.

Both A—— and G—— lived to be " recov-

ered out of the snare of the devil," to enter the
ministry of the gospel, although late in life,
and to give some years of self-denying toil to
the Master whom they had dishonored. But
they had "pierced themselves through with
many sorrows," whose memory never left them
nor ever ceased to be bitter; and the unsightly
scars remained.

There is scarcely a doubt that the full an-
nals of Christian experience, in our own land
and time alone, would tell of thousands who,
through neglecting to follow the Light of life,
"have erred from the faith and pierced themselves through."

> "Nothing but leaves!
> The Spirit grieves
> Over a wasted life,
> O'er sins committed while conscience slept,
> Promises made, but never kept, —
> Folly, and sin, and shame.
> Nothing but leaves! Nothing but leaves!"

IV.

REPROVED AND RECALLED.

"Be not conformed to this world."—Rom. xii. 2.

"Ye are all the children of Light and the children of the day; we are not of the night, nor of darkness. Therefore let us not sleep as do others, but let us watch, and be sober."— 1 Thess. v. 5, 6.

SOME object to the denunciation of worldliness *as* worldliness. They say it implies an antagonism between the world and Christ which does not exist.

In modern days, there has arisen a new philosophy of Christian duty as it regards "the world." Advocates of this philosophy select as their motto the half-verse, "In the world," entirely omitting the complementary half, "but not of the world." They affect the phrases, — "Christian worldliness," "practical Christianity," "the nobility of man," "culture," "the tendencies of the times," "the best modern thought," "the glory of the nineteenth century," "the church of the future." They overpraise the moralist, and depreciate the evangelist. They put a slight upon the requisition of church-membership, disparage dogma and creeds, and merge faith in fidelity, and love to God in love to man. They confound Christian worship with Christian work, and impute both to some men who never worship, and who reject Christ. They slight the prophecies which foretell a change in the present order of things through great convulsions. They tone down the startling statements, the humbling doctrines, and the exacting requirements of the Scriptures. And, in general, they endeavor to bridge the gulf, to close the chasm, and to effect a compromising union between Christianity and "the world." Then they tell us that *this* scheme of Christian living is *practicable !* — The offensive implication is evident.

This philosophy undoubtedly had its origin, as has every plausible error, in an examination of certain facts; but not all the pertinent facts were viewed, and the few considered were be-

held in other light than that which the Scriptures afford.

It is a fact that the world is better in many of
its appearances and its acts than it once was,
for we see more active charity (in the secondary
sense of the term), and a habit that is less
grossly rude and coarse, than the olden time
disclosed. It is also true that unconverted men
are not always wanting in amiable feeling and
heroic endeavor; that Holy Writ tells of a coming day of universal purity; and, that meanwhile the disciples of Christ are bidden to live
and work among men.

But there are other facts quite as pertinent
and quite as well ascertained, demanding place
in the induction of any theory of Christian duty.
These have been ignored; and by a partial induction, necessarily erroneous, these modern
theorists assume to have established the general principles, — that " the world " itself is, or
is becoming a friend to Truth; that its native
tendency now, is upward; and that the best
evangelistic work will not henceforth hold up

the church as something apart from and above " the world."

There is an unpleasant significance in the fact that this philosophy, shorn perhaps of its more repulsive features, finds wide — although happily, not general — acceptance among the churches.

The Scriptures must decide this matter. What is their testimony?

It will be found that the expressions " the world," " this world," and " this present world," are convertible terms, used widely and with an unbroken consistency in the Scriptures, in what some will deem a technical sense. It will become evident that they are meant to characterize an entity, a spiritual influence and force, which is at deadly enmity with the Saviour of sinners.

Some passages declare this enmity : —

"The world cannot hate you,* but me it hateth, because I testify of it that *the works thereof are evil.*"

* *You,* — the brethren of Jesus according to the flesh; not his disciples.

"If the world hate you, ye know that it hated me before it hated you."

"And the world hath hated them, because they are not of the world, even as I am not of the world."

"Know ye not that the friendship of the world is enmity with God?"

"For all that is in the world, the lust of the flesh, the lust of the eye, and the pride of life, is not of the Father, but of the world."

These teachings imply, at least, that the followers of Jesus are to expect the same hostility which it is declared the world visits upon Him; and that, while evangelically loving men and seeking to save them *out of* "the world," they are not to strike hands in unholy friendship with this enemy. Other teachings are more explicit:—

"And we have received, not the spirit of the world, but the spirit which is of God."

"Therefore the world knoweth us not, because it knew Him not."

"A little while, and the world seeth me no more; but ye see me."

"If ye were of the world, the world would love his own; but because ye are not of the world, but I have chosen you out of the world, therefore the world hateth you."

" A little while, and the world shall not see me ; . . . ye shall weep and lament, but the world shall rejoice."

" Do ye not know that the saints shall judge the world ? "

" But God forbid that I should glory, save in the cross of our Lord Jesus Christ, by whom the world is crucified unto me, and I unto the world."

" *Know ye not that the friendship of the world is enmity with God? Whosoever therefore will be a friend of the world is the enemy of God!*"

" Ye are of God, little children. . . . They are of the world."

" Love not the world, neither the things of the world. If any man love the world, the love of the Father is not in him."

" Pure religion and undefiled before God and the Father, is this : to visit the fatherless and widows in their affliction, and to keep himself unspotted from the world."

" Be not conformed to this world ; but be ye transformed by the renewing of your mind, that ye may prove what is that good, and acceptable, and perfect will of God."

H

" And you hath He quickened who were dead in trespasses and sins, wherein in time past ye walked, according to the course of this world."

" For Demas hath forsaken us, having loved this present world."

" . . . who gave himself for us that He might redeem us from all iniquity, and purify unto himself *a peculiar people* zealous of good works."

" But ye are a chosen generation, a royal priesthood, a holy nation, a peculiar people; that ye should show forth the praises of Him who hath called you out of darkness into His marvellous light."

" Ye are all the children of Light and the children of the day; we are not of the night nor of darkness. Therefore let us not sleep as do others."

" Be ye not unequally yoked with unbelievers; . . . what communion hath Light with darkness?"

" The Light shineth in darkness."

" Let us therefore cast off the works of darkness, and let us put on the armor of Light."

" For ye were sometime darkness, but now are ye Light in the Lord; walk as children of Light. . . . And have no fellowship with the unfruitful works of darkness, but rather reprove them."

In order to make the contrast and the duty more evident, the Scriptures vividly portray the

ruin and degradation of " this world " as such,
and distinctly name the vicious rule which holds
it subject : —

" But when *we* are judged, we are chastened of the
Lord, that we should not be *condemned with the world.*"

" And we know that we are of God ; and the whole
world lieth in the wicked one." *

" . . . wherein in time past ye walked, according to
the course of this world; according to the Prince of
the power of the air, the spirit that now worketh in the
children of disobedience."

" The god of this world hath blinded the minds of
them that believe not."

" And the great dragon was cast out, that old serpent, called the Devil, and Satan, which deceiveth the
whole world."

" . . . the rulers of the darkness of this world."

" For the Prince of this world cometh."

" . . . because the Prince of this world is judged."

There is, then, an antagonism between the
spirit of " this world " and the spirit of Christ ;
an antagonism not accidental and temporary,

* " *Wicked one*" for " wickedness " as commonly read.
The former is generally conceded to be the correct translation.

but essential; and as permanent, at least, as the need of Christians for New Testament instruction.

The words still stand, "ye are not of this world," "they are not of this world, but I have chosen them out of the world." Christians are called to be "a holy nation," "a peculiar people;" to be followers of Christ, not of men; to walk in the Light, not in darkness. We are surrounded by darkness, by unseen foes. Temptations beset us at every point and in every form. Pitfalls abound. It is easy to stumble. The only safety lies in turning a deaf ear to the suggestions of men except as they are found, upon inquiry, to express the commands of God; in turning from all guides but Jesus Christ. There can be no substantial or abiding peace, no adequate usefulness until, at whatever cost, the whole life be surrendered to, and guided by, the requirements of the Master through the utterances of His Word.

PART THIRD.

STANDING IN THE LIGHT.

(Christian Knowledge.)

"My people are destroyed for lack of knowledge. — Hos. iv. 6.

"But grow in grace and the knowledge of our Lord and Saviour Jesus Christ."—1 PET. iii. 18.

I.

LEARNING TO SEE.

"The entrance of thy words giveth light."—Ps. cxix. 130.

ONE who suddenly emerges from great darkness is dazzled. At first he sees nothing clearly. He does not know at what to look: all objects present themselves in a confused mass, and a mist seems to surround them all.

A blind man, healed by the Saviour, said: "I see men as trees walking." "After that He put His hands again upon his eyes and made him look up; and he was restored, and saw every man clearly."

This man had evidently *become* blind; he had seen before; otherwise he had not been so ready in the use of his vision.

A young girl, blind from her early infancy, whose sight was restored, was taken to her own room where she knew every article familiarly by touch. There the bandages were taken from her eyes. At first she feared to move lest she should run against some object, or to raise her hand lest she should strike it; every thing seemed so near. She asked the name of every thing. She knew nothing by sight. She made the most absurd mistakes. Her knowledge before had been the defective knowledge of " darkness," and was of no direct avail to her "in the light." It proved of indirect use only, as she opened and closed her eyes by turns, using the touch and then the vision, and comparing results.

The young Christian encounters a similar difficulty. The two cases are analogous in every detail named. For —

" If any man be in Christ, he is a new creature; old things are passed away; behold all things are become new ! "

A new Light shines. A new radiance rests on the commonest duties and relationships of life. A glow suffuses .the whole atmosphere.

But the eye does not discriminate at first. Objects and relationships are not distinguished. The paths are not at once discerned. The conditions of the life are so completely changed, the knowledge is to be gained in a method so utterly new, that the soul is tempted either to close the eyes again and walk " by touch," by past habit, or to shrink back, timorous and confused.

Every thing is to be learned. That knowledge of Christ which is needed for practical guidance is not inborn : it must be acquired by patient process. Immediately following the invitation to the sinner, " Come unto me, . . . and I will give you rest," we find the command to the young believer, " Take my yoke upon you and *learn of me*, . . . and *ye shall find* rest unto your souls."

The Christian must needs learn how to use the Scriptures, which afford the light that is to be his constant guide. He must learn how to procure their direction most advantageously; upon questions of thought about God, about the

6

soul's standing in His sight, about men and their necessities; and upon questions of opinion and duty in general.

Even this knowledge cannot be acquired at second hand. One must study the Scriptures in order to learn how to study them. "Practice makes perfect." One learns to swim only in the water. The disciple must go straight to the Master.

All that is said in these pages is designed to stimulate to, and to aid in, this study of God's word; not to supplant it, even to the slightest extent.

A Christian minister once said of "The Witness," a religious periodical published by the late James Inglis, that he liked it because it always spurred him to study of the Word.

After a prolonged interview between two clergymen, the younger said: "I enjoyed the interview. I never before heard so much pertinent quotation from the Scriptures. I shall go to my Bible with new zest."

This is the true aim of all human address, to

point to the Light; that, in the Light and using
the Light, one may *learn* to use it, to discern
the revelations which it makes, and to walk in
the path which it illumines.

THE FELLOWSHIP OF LIGHT.

"But if we walk in the Light, as He is in the light, we have fellowship one with another." "And truly our fellowship is with the Father, and His Son Jesus Christ." — 1 JOHN i. 3, 7.

SLIGHT as seems the act by which the man becomes a Christian, he by it leaps an immeasurable gulf. The contrast between his present and his past position is more than striking: it is startling!

"Ye were sometime *darkness*, but now are ye *light*."

"Ye who . . . were *far off*, are made *nigh*."

"Ye are no more *strangers*, but *fellow-citizens of the saints*."

"He that believeth not *is condemned*." "He that believeth . . . *hath life*."

"And you who were *dead* hath He *quickened*."

"He that . . . believeth . . . is passed from *death* unto *life*."

The common notion is, that the Christian is but an ordinary man with a slight and pleasing difference, — an added vague and uncertain hope, an added feeble motive, and some small aids to a better life and a purer character.

Those whose thought is on so low a plane will not experience the thrill which these injunctions hold concealed : —

"I therefore, the prisoner of the Lord, beseech you that ye walk *worthy of the vocation* wherewith ye are called."

" . . . That ye might walk worthy of the Lord."

" . . . That ye should walk worthy of God, who hath called you into His kingdom and glory."

A rich man has usually but small temptation to go about in rags, begging. It is only he who supposes that he has received but the petty gift of a day's food, a single garment, or a distant and uncertain promise merely, who deems himself still wretched and needy, and associates freely with the lazzaroni. The Christian whose conceptions of his position, companionships, and prospects are low and degrading, is apt to conform himself to the world: the separation seems scarcely more than nominal, and the descent is easy and natural.

The common talk of a large class of Christians

is full of lamentation. The best they can say of their new life is, that it is subject to great vicissitudes. They seem to have the rare and unenviable faculty of extracting gloom from the brightest things, — from the Gospel itself with all its precious promises and its alluring revelations. They revel in " the tribulations," " the temptations," " the dangers." They hug their doubts. They even seem in some strange way to enjoy their distress! They shun the Light as if they feared it would hurt them.

This is a mischievous travesty of true Christian experience. Christianity was designed to make men glad. The annunciation was emphatic: " Fear not! for behold I bring you glad tidings of great joy." Our Saviour's pathway was not left strewn with inconsolable penitents, but adorned with gladdened hearts. The returning prodigal was welcomed *at once* to the arms of a loving father, and was promptly crowned with the joy of a child at home and the honor due an accepted and beloved son. And the Scriptures repeatedly enjoin Christians to "praise the Lord," to "be glad in the Lord," to "rejoice alway," and to "joy in God."

What, less than this, could be the significance of the prophetic words appropriated by the Saviour? —

"The Lord hath appointed me to preach good tidings unto the meek; He hath sent me to bind up the broken-hearted, to proclaim liberty to the captives, . . . to appoint unto them that mourn in Zion, to give unto them the oil of joy for mourning, the garment of praise for the spirit of heaviness."

It is only a distortion or a neglect of the Gospel that can make the condition of the believer other than enviable: the gloomy either do not know the promises, or they put dishonor on them and make "God a liar."

The Scriptures assure the Christian that he enjoys a position of rare exaltation and security.

1. He is in fellowship with the saints: "Now therefore ye are no more strangers and foreigners, but fellow-citizens of the saints and of the household of God."

There is an equality in the republic of grace.

We constitute a kingdom only as Christ is King, — "and we shall reign with Him!" There are no titled nobility as "bulwarks to the throne." The humblest believer is in full standing in the brotherhood. Said the Rev. Dr. —— to a young clergyman who held him in high esteem and was disposed to "look up" to him : —

"Why do you always call me Doctor? Why not say 'Brother,' sometimes at least, that we may keep in mind our brotherhood and our equality in grace."

Paul, writing to the churches, addressed himself "to the saints," "to the saints of God." His letters betray the existence of evils among the people to whom he wrote, akin to those which disfigure the Christian profession to-day. Some were guilty of shameful folly even. But all were "saints:" no discrimination was admissible.

The youngest, the feeblest, the most wayward Christian is in full fellowship with the household of God. His standing before God is in Jesus, not in himself. Only "by the blood of Jesus" are we "brought nigh" and redeemed from alienage. In Christ all must stand alike. "Is Christ divided?" The pitiful attainments of the flesh, even Christian growth and toil, avail nothing in giving us standing before God. That standing is a *gift;* it is bestowed once for all, and fully, upon the soul's first act of faith: "Ye *are* complete in Him."

The promises, precepts, warnings, counsels, names, which the Scriptures give to "saints," are for all. The acceptance of Christ puts the soul "in Him," where are all the saints, and gives to each the fellowship of all the rest, with all the dignity and the equality, and with a right to all the sympathy, implied in a fellowship so exalted and intimate.

This is the fellowship of saved souls. The Christian is saved! His destiny is secure.

At an inquiry meeting a young man was thus addressed: —

"May I ask whether you are saved?"

"Saved! I cannot say that I am. If I could, I dare say I should not be here to-night. But, begging your pardon, sir, how can any man say

6* I

he is saved? Is it not the height of presumption to say so?"

How so, when the Scriptures avow the design of bringing men to this knowledge? — " These things have I written unto you that believe on the name of the Son of God, that ye may know that ye have eternal life." The presumption is, the rather, in declining to be brought to this knowledge, in doubting God's word. He has said : —

" He that believeth on the Son hath life."

" He that heareth my word, and believeth on Him that sent me, hath everlasting life and shall not come into condemnation ; but is passed from death unto life."

" He that believeth on me hath everlasting life."

One may not "feel" all this as true in his case. But this is God's testimony ; what right has man to indulge his "thoughts" or to cling to his "feelings," when they contradict God's word? Does man know better than God? — "He that believeth not God hath made Him a liar !"

A gentleman who had a vinery took a friend

who called upon him to see it. The sun was very strong, and the place was very hot. His friend remarked upon the temperature, and asked if it were not heated artificially. He was told that it was not. On coming out he was observed putting down his hand to *feel* the pipes! This was making his friend a liar; he insulted him, although not intentionally, by not believing him; and, it may be added, by relying on his "feelings" as against his friend's word, where that word was designed to be final testimony.*

There was a trace of excuse for this unbelief: man may prove false. But how shall we doubt God? His statements are repeated and plain: *the believing soul is saved.*

True, the Christian stumbles. He is weak. "We have this treasure in earthen vessels." One needs daily to offer the prayer, "Forgive us our debts." But —

"If we confess our sins, God is faithful and just to forgive us our sins, and to cleanse us from all unrighteousness."

* From "Life and Light."

"By Him all that believe are justified from all things. . . . "

God is pledged. He will be faithful to His promises, and just to His Son — in whom the believer stands :—

"Of Him are ye in Christ Jesus, who of God is made unto us wisdom, and righteousness, and sanctification, and redemption."

"As He is so *are* we in this world."

"By grace *are* ye saved, through faith."

After the sense of guilt, comes the sense of lust. It is a moment of keen pain and of a horror of dread when the Christian, perhaps after years of unsuspecting ignorance, awakes to the consciousness of powerful indwelling lust. The unfathomed chasm of iniquity filled with unnamed horrors which suddenly opens at his feet, and especially the knowledge that he cannot measure his depravity or fully discover the possibilities of his "carnal mind" in crime, may well sink the soul in shame and wrap it up in a nameless dread, until the thought of Christ steal in.

The alarmed believer may well cry out with Paul: "O wretched man that I am! *who shall deliver me from the body of this death?*" But, being a believer, he may not justly fail to continue with the apostle, in the triumphant burst of assurance: "I thank *God*, through Jesus Christ my Lord!" Nor should he decline or neglect to continue in the word still further, to appropriate the sequence, — the delightful assurances of the passage * which immediately follows; nor should he cease his study of this apt and cheering word, though he ponder it once and again with ear attent to the Master's voice, until the closing burst of exultation seem all his own: —

"What shall we say then? If God be for us, who can be against us? He that spared not His own Son, · but delivered Him up for us all, how shall He not with Him freely give us all things? *Who shall lay any thing to the charge of God's elect!* It is God that justifieth, who is he that condemneth! Who . . . shall separate us from the love of Christ? Shall tribulation, or distress . . . ? Nay, in all these things we

* Romans viii.

are more than conquerors through Him that loved us. For I am persuaded that neither death, nor life, nor angels, nor principalities, nor powers, nor things present, nor things to come, nor height, nor depth, nor any other creature, shall be able to separate us from the love of God which is in Christ Jesus our Lord."

What more could be said! Yet this is God's testimony to every believer.

Many Christians fail to receive this testimony. Why? The light is too dazzling for weak eyes. The news seems " too good to be true."

" It is said that Captain Barclay . . . once laid a wager of £500 with another gentleman, who did not know human nature so well as himself, that he would not sell twenty sovereigns in an hour on London bridge at a penny each. The coins were procured, and the man to sell them. He stood holding one up, crying: ' Genuine gold! genuine gold! only a penny each.' But the people rushed past him, either taking no heed, or laughing at him, concluding it must be a dodge. At last, within a few minutes of the expiration of the hour, a humble working-man passed who was out of employment at the time. He stopped, he looked, he bought one and saw that it was indeed genuine gold. He had only another sixpence in his pocket. He bought the sixpence worth, and ran away to get more money. When he returned the man had gone. He had sold only the seven. Why? Because 'a sovereign for a penny' was too good news to be true!" *

God gives life "without money and without price." Few take it; and of those who do, few realize the greatness or even the reality of the gift.

"A rich man in England lately became a Christian, and began to speak to others. He thought every one would believe him, it was all so clear to him; but he found it otherwise. Among other things he did to learn human nature and the principles of unbelief, he hired an empty house in a town and put up placards to the effect that any one belonging to that town who was in debt would get money to pay

* From "Life and Light."

it on a given day between the hours of nine and
ten. The people laughed and called it a hoax.
At half-past nine of the day named, a poor man
crept slowly along to the door. On entering
and learning that it was no hoax, he told all
about his debts and got money to pay them. A
very few more came, all small debtors. He gave
them the money, amounting only to £200; but
kept them all until ten o'clock, when he shut
the door and preached Jesus to them. He then
let them away. The news soon got abroad. A
rush was made upon the house; but 'the door
was shut!' It was past the hour." *

It is marvellous what incredulity men display in the presence of God's repeated and distinct assertions. It is most marvellous that
Christians, who have ventured upon His word,
should still doubt it. Their incredulity, however, does not change the facts: it serves only
to mar their happiness, to paralyze effort, and to
put dishonor on the Cross.

Two ladies entered a railway car together at

* From "Life and Light."

G——, provided with tickets for the city of C——. Two roads cross at that point, four trains set out in as many different directions at about the same time, and passengers daily board the wrong train. The ladies were in doubt. The conductor entered, wearing his badge.

" Is this the train for C—— ? "

" Yes," was the reply, prompt and distinct. The train soon started. The tickets were collected. One of the ladies was at her ease, and evidently enjoyed the travel. The other, unused to journeys and suspicious of men, was in a continual fret. She reached her destination as quickly and as safely as the other ! But the eight hours of interval, which should have furnished enjoyment, yielded only discomfort to herself and annoyance to those about her.

There is nothing but God's word to rest upon. That word assures us that the believing soul is saved. Why should not the Christian on this testimony know his security, enjoy his heritage of peace and gladness, and be spurred to exertion?

2. There is something beyond this, however. The believer has fellowship with the Father, and with His Son Jesus Christ: —

"That which we have seen and heard declare we unto you that ye may have fellowship with us ; and truly our fellowship is with the Father, and with His Son Jesus Christ."

The returning prodigal thought to enter his father's home as a servant: he was welcomed and honored as a son. The believer is a son of God. The distinction indicated by this name is not merely nominal: it is vital: —

"But to them that received Him, to them gave He power to become the sons of God."

"Behold what manner of love the Father hath bestowed upon us, that we should be called the sons of God!"

"Beloved, now are we the sons of God."

This sonship is not by adoption *alone :* it is by birth also. It brings with it all the privileges and the present standing which this fact suggests ; a dignity, a wealth of privilege, which it staggers the Christian to contemplate as his own — his own *now :* —

" . . . to them gave He power to become the sons of God, which were born . . . of God."

"I am dead; nevertheless I live; yet not I, but Christ liveth in me."

" . . . whereby are given unto us exceeding great and precious promises, that by them ye might be partakers of the divine nature."

" For both He that sanctifieth and they which are sanctified are all of One; for which cause He is not ashamed to call them brethren."

Hence the Christian is a brother of Jesus "in full blood," "begotten of God" by the same Spirit and partaking of the same nature. Thus he is an heir of God : —

"And if children, then heirs ; heirs of God, joint-heirs with Christ; if so be that we suffer with Him, that we may be also glorified *together*."

It is thus that it becomes literally true, as the Scriptures assert, that : —

" Our citizenship * is in heaven."

" God . . . hath . . . made us sit together in heavenly places in Christ Jesus."

---

* Phil. iii. 20. This is conceded to be the correct translation.

" Here we have no continuing city, but we seek one to come."

The Christian is a pilgrim here. His home is in heaven. It is there his Saviour dwells, in whom he stands, who is his Life. There Christ maintains his place until He shall present him faultless before the Father. While he dwells on earth absent from home, hampered by indwelling sin, walking by faith, seeing "through a glass darkly," often forgetting and often falling, his place is kept. It is written : —

"These things write I unto you that ye sin not; and if any man sin, we have an Advocate with the Father, Jesus Christ the righteous."

He guarantees the eternal inheritance promised. *In Him* it is already conveyed! It belongs to the Christian; the title is in his possession, in the promises of the Word; the token of transfer is the blood; there is no condition attached save that already fulfilled, — the soul's acceptance of Christ. Nothing can occur to wrest this inheritance from him. The guarantee is not in the firmness and persistence of the soul's hold on Christ, but in the tenacity of His grasp upon His saints: —

" I know my sheep . . . ; and they shall never perish ; neither shall any man pluck them out of my hand. My Father which gave them me is greater than all, and no man is able to pluck them out of my Father's hand."

" Those whom thou hast given me I have kept ; and none of them is lost ;* but the son of perdition [is lost], that the Scripture might be fulfilled."

A young man once greeted a clergyman with this boast : " I am a happy man. I am safe. I have hold of the Cross *with both hands !* And I am not going to let go." "What if Satan should cut off your hands !" was the discriminating reply. The boaster was staggered. He had had faith in his faith, not faith in Christ. He is not now numbered among Christians. Paul's statement is : —

* This seems to be the more correct punctuation. "But" (εἰ μή), as here used, *sets off* what follows in a new category. *See* Luke iv. 25–27; there the widow of *Sidon,* is set off by " save" (εἰ μή) from "many widows . . . in *Israel;* " and Naaman the *Syrian,* by "saving" (εἰ μή again) from "many lepers . . . in *Israel.*" There is a *contrast* in each case.

"I follow after, if that I *may* apprehend * that for which also I *am* apprehended of Christ Jesus."

"For ye are dead; and your life is *hid* with Christ in God."

Our redemption is in Christ — is Christ. "He that hath the Son hath life." "For He *is* your life." This is not manifest, visible, although true; but, "When He who is your Life shall appear, *then* shall ye also appear with Him in glory." The Christian is in Christ now; he shall so "appear" then. The fact is present; only its manifestation tarries. If the Christian walk by sight, he realizes nothing of this glory; but "we walk by faith, *not* by sight!" We know, now.

Thus "looking" out of self, away from men and "unto Jesus," the Christian learns that, *in Him*, his fellowship is and shall ever be "with the Father and His Son Jesus Christ." It is thus that God has done for the believer the identical thing prayed for by a Christian in France: —

* *Apprehend,* take hold of; *apprehended of,* taken hold of by.

" Lord, save me from myself,
    And save me in spite of myself,
    And take me out of myself,
    For Jesus Christ's sake.   Amen."

The Christian's " walk " may be far below
this dignity.   It is always needful to pray, as
we sing : —

" *Nearer*, my God, to thee."

The explicit injunction of the Word is : " I
beseech you therefore, brethren, that ye walk
worthy of the vocation wherewith ye are called."
And Paul thus names his own effort : " I *press
toward* the mark for the prize of the high calling
of God in Christ Jesus."

This endeavor must be made, with exertion
constant and unflagging.   To it Christians are
everywhere incited.   It is designed to supply
the needed motive, the motive of self-respect at
least, by revealing this high calling and this
matchless companionship.   It is because Christians are " the children of Light " that they are
exhorted : " Walk as children of Light."   The
" being " precedes the walk, and is not im-
peached by a thousand failures in the attempt.

" For ye were sometime darkness, but now are ye light in the Lord; [therefore] walk as children of Light."

The transition is already made. Behold the present, then look back upon the past. Behold the sinner, then look upon the Christian : —

"A yawning gulf spreads out between !"

3. The Christian has fellowship also with the Holy Ghost : —

"If there be therefore any consolation in Christ, if any comfort of love, if any fellowship of the Spirit. . . ."

" The grace of our Lord Jesus Christ, the love of God, and the communion of the Holy Ghost be with you all.   Amen."

" For He dwelleth with you and shall be in you."

" Know ye not that ye are the temple of God, and that the Spirit of God dwelleth in you ? "

" Now if any man have not the Spirit of Christ he is none of His."

Had not the Spirit entered the heart, not one passage of Scripture had thrown its light upon the believer's path.   Until He come, —

" . . . the god of this world hath blinded the minds of them that believe not, lest the light of the glorious gospel of Christ, who is the image of God, should shine unto them."

God's word concerning all spiritual movement, whether toward the truth or in the truth, is that it is " not by might, nor by power, but by my Spirit." The soul was dead; it is now alive: " You who were dead hath He quickened." He who accepts Christ does so through the operations of the Holy Ghost: " To them gave he power to believe . . . which were born . . . of God." And the same testimony assures us that where He takes up His abode, there He remains: " . . . the Holy Spirit of God whereby ye are sealed unto the day of redemption."

The presence of the Holy Ghost in the soul is the earnest of redemption : —

"In whom, also, after that ye believed, ye were sealed with the Holy Spirit of promise, which is the earnest of our inheritance until the redemption of the purchased possession."

"Who also hath given unto us the earnest of the Spirit. Wherefore we are always confident . . . "

"Who hath also sealed us and given us the earnest of the Spirit in our hearts."

"Earnest" is foretaste. The day of redemption will bring the full realization of Christ: "We know that when He shall appear, we shall be like Him." This is the essential feature of future bliss ; the character, not the surroundings : "I shall be satisfied when I awake with thy likeness." Of this bliss the present Spirit is the foretaste ; by Him Christ now liveth in us and something of heavenly felicity is experienced. As His operations proceed, the "earnest" becomes more patent to the soul: as by Him the soul appropriates more of Christ and lives by faith more fully, the foretaste imperceptibly changes into a constant feast. This is feeding on Christ. The Spirit conducts this work ; so He is the earnest, affords the foretaste, of the heavenly realization. "Earnest" is not "token," to be examined, Watts' hymn to the contrary notwithstanding —

" . . . descend and bring some token of thy grace."

The Spirit is unseen of man. His presence is not to be detected by probing the heart in search for Him. He worketh where He listeth, and His footsteps — like the origin and destiny of the wind — are beyond the reach of our discoveries. We know His presence, first and chiefly, by God's testimony through the Word; then, also, by its fruits in knowledge of the Scriptures, and the like.

" For we have not received the Spirit of bondage again to fear, but we have received the Spirit of adoption, whereby we cry Abba,* Father. For the Spirit itself beareth witness with our spirit that we are the children of God."

This " witness " does not find utterance by *soliloquy* of the heart, but by the voice of Scripture quickened by the Spirit and spoken *in* the heart. This is no " token," no inner

---

* *Abba*, a Syriac word for " father," said to be a term of familiarity and endearment. By the Spirit we come to know God familiarly, as our Father, " Abba."

The child familiarly says " papa," rather than " father." Is there not a significance in the similarity of the two words " Abba," " papa " ?

feeling, but the junction of the heart and the word of promise in sympathetic union. The " witness " appears, or is heard, only as the Word is employed.

The ability to grasp but a single promise, however feebly ; even the recognition of the law and its condemnation — though every promise seem to take wing — is proof that the Spirit is at work upon the soul. No "token " is needed to supplement this testimony.

When, in a crowd, one is impelled further, faster, or in another direction, than he had intended going or had before been able to go, it is evident that some one has given him a push, even though the actor be not discovered nor the distinct impress of his hand felt.

On God's testimony, then, the believer is assured that the Holy Spirit is now and henceforth his constant and most intimate companion, dwelling *in* him and able to work by night and by day for his advancement and his comfort in the divine life. Upon this fact is based the exhortation : —

" Grieve not the Holy Spirit of God, whereby ye are sealed unto the day of redemption."

The word is not, "Grieve Him not away." He will not go! although some strangely fear He may." " . . . sealed unto the day of redemption" is the word: the seal cannot be removed. Sin may obscure the Presence, but cannot banish it.

" Grieve Him not ; " as if it were said : He is your companion, your helper, your friend ; do not grieve him by sin, by turning a deaf ear to the Word, by plunging into the companionships of vice, by compelling Him as your constant companion to go into the midst of uncongenial scenes and unfriendly associations, by filling your soul — where He has His seat — with lustful thoughts and carnal desires.

This companionship may prove a source of delight. It will lend a glow to the Scriptures. It will fit the soul for the profitable use of the ordinances of God's house. It will yield pleasure through the fellowship of the brethren. It will suggest agreeable and profitable medita-

tions, stimulate the soul in its aspirations, lend
vigor to the warnings of conscience upon the
approach of sin, and keep the judgment clear in
deciding questions of duty. In general, it will
lead the soul away from sin and develop the
budding divine life, ministering to it the joy of
the sweetest, most congenial, most profitable,
most intimate, most constant fellowship possible,
— the fellowship of the saints and the fellowship of the Father and the Son, of which the
Spirit is the sole Agent.

> "I've found a joy in sorrow,
>   A secret balm for pain;
> A beautiful to-morrow
>   Of sunshine, after rain;
> I've found a branch of healing
>   Near every bitter spring;
> A whispered promise, stealing
>   O'er every broken string!
> .   .   .   .
> "My Saviour! thee possessing,
>   We have the joy, the balm;
> The healing and the blessing,
>   The sunshine and the psalm;
> The promise for the fearful,
>   The Elim for the faint,
> The rainbow for the tearful,
>   The *glory* for the saint!"

III.

THE SECRET OF LIGHT.

"The secret of the Lord is with them that fear Him."
Ps. xxv. 14.

THERE is a little lake, nestled among the hills, whose bosom is always placid and whose waters are always clear, which yet has no visible source of supply. It is fed by hidden streams.

There is a river in one of our Western States whose waters until recently were singularly pure, whose volume varied comparatively little throughout the year, and whose temperature, even, seemed in some degree exempt from the influences of the seasons. To an extent not easily ascertained, it is supplied by springs from the rocks beneath. It is not inappropriately named *Rock* River. Latterly Art has wrought vast disturbance with Nature; the hand of man in agriculture and manufactures has brought a change and a contamination; yet the peculiar features indicated, although less marked, are still to be observed.

Nature lacks reinforcement by fresh creative acts; yet even here there is a concealed power which retains sway amid the imported disturbances of human life. How much more shall Grace, daily reinforced from above, through secret channels, bear rule in the midst of the most absorbing care!

The Psalmist says: "There is a river the streams whereof shall make glad the city of God;" and a judicious commentator* thus annotates: "The streams of spiritual blessings flowing from God through Jesus Christ, make glad the city of God continually." The apostle, speaking of the fathers, says "they did all eat the same spiritual meat and did all drink the same spiritual drink; for they drank of that spiritual Rock which followed them; and that Rock was Christ."

The Christian life depends upon a hidden

* Rev. W. S. Plumer, D.D.

source of supply. There is a *secret* in it. There is a mystical union between the risen Christ in heaven, and the believer on earth. His prayer for us was, and is: " That they all may be one ; as thou, Father, art in me, and I in thee, that they also may be one in us." Elsewhere He says : " I am the vine, ye are the branches. . . . Abide in me. As the branch cannot bear fruit of itself except it abide in the vine, no more can ye, except ye abide in me. . . . He that abideth in me, and I in him, the same bringeth forth much fruit; for without me ye can do nothing."

" The secret of holy living lies in this doctrine of the union of the believer with Christ. This is not only the ground of his hope of pardon, but the source of the strength whereby he dies unto sin and lives unto righteousness. It is by being rooted and grounded in Christ that he is strengthened with might in the inner man, and is enabled to comprehend the breadth and length and depth and height of the mystery of redemption, and to know the love of God which passeth knowledge, and is filled with all the fulness of God. It is this doctrine which sustains him under all his trials,

7*

and enables him to triumph over all his enemies, for it is not he that lives, but Christ that lives in him, giving him grace sufficient for his day, and purifying him unto Himself as one of His peculiar people zealous of good works.

"As union with Christ is the source of spiritual life, the means by which that life is maintained and promoted are all related to this doctrine and derive from it their efficacy." *

It is surely a delightful thing that the soul has its secret with the Lord, is in His secret counsels, is permitted to approach Him in secret, and hides in secret all the operations of the inner life, — its flow to and through the soul. The nearness of approach, the intimacy, the sacred friendship and fellowship which these

---

* Dr. Charles Hodge in "The Way of Life." If it may be permitted to venture upon a modification of the language employed by one so learned and usually so accurate, let it be suggested that the form is put for the fact wherever the word "doctrine" is used in the passage quoted. The doctrine, the teaching, is valuable; but "the secret of holy living lies" not in the "doctrine," but in the *fact* of the believers' union with Christ. And so elsewhere. It is this use of the word "doctrine" which leads some men to say we make creeds every thing. Dr. Hodge puts it right when he says: "As *union* with Christ is the source," &c.

facts suggest, are fitted to bathe the soul in pleasure, in sweet humility in view of its exaltation, and in the baptism of holy love.

"The secret of the Lord is with them that fear Him."

"His secret is with the righteous."

"Enter into thy closet, and pray to thy Father which is in secret."

"In the secret of His tabernacle shall He hide me."

"He revealeth His secrets unto His servants."

"Henceforth I call you not servants; for the servant knoweth not what his lord doeth: but I have called you friends; for all things that I have heard of my Father I have made known unto you."

The second chapter of Paul's first letter to the Corinthians is devoted entirely to this pleasing subject: —

"Howbeit we speak wisdom among them that are perfect; yet not the wisdom of this world, nor of the princes of this world, that come to nought: but we speak the wisdom of God in a mystery, even the hidden wisdom, which God ordained before the world unto our glory; which none of the princes of this world knew; . . . as it is written, Eye hath not seen, nor ear heard, neither have entered into the heart *of man*, the things which God hath prepared for them that love Him. *But God hath revealed them unto us by His Spirit; . . .* the things of God knoweth no man, but the Spirit of God. Now *we have received . . . the Spirit of God; that we might know* the things that are freely given to us of God; . . . we have the mind of Christ."

Surely here, standing in the light, there opens before the eyes a vista of pleasant things rich in promise — nay in the fruition — of sweetness, strength, and comfort. The humblest believer is rich, in Christ. He *hath* Christ. A secret channel of communication conducts his thoughts away to the ear of his listening Lord, and brings back His thoughts to enrich the soul. Prayer carries the soul's thought up: the Scriptures bear Christ's thought back. Men may hear the prayer, but they little know the secret thought it conveys. Men read the Bible; but only the believing heart receives the peculiar messages it brings. All is secret.

This " subterranean channel " is the Holy Spirit, the agent of God in imparting the divine life to the soul and in reinforcing it there ; and the agent of the soul in seeking God's face, whether by prayer, by praise, or by any other means of grace which he may employ. The Spirit of God is with God, is God ; He also dwells in man ; and so He sweetly, subtly, and effectually binds the two in ONE, not by external bonds, but in a living union like that which unites the branch to the vine ; a union of such a nature that the streams of desire and of supply flow through it, back and forth, — like the blood through the veins and arteries, — unrevealed to the gaze of men and unhindered by the foes of the soul.

It is *thus* that the believer has a present and fruitful fellowship in heavenly places, " with the Father, and with His Son Jesus Christ : " " He shall receive of mine, and shall show it unto you."

It is thus that Christ executes His guarantee, keeping the soul that has committed itself to Him. He *dwells* within the heart by faith, through His Spirit.

It is thus that our destiny is linked in eternal and vital union with that of Christ; it is thus that we are now linked with Him in glory, although we daily trail our robes in the mire; · with His safety, although we are surrounded by perils; with His acceptance in the Father's presence, although we often sin; with His glorious manhood, although we are foolish and frail: " As He is, so are we in this world." Whatever He is, we are. His suffering for sin is ours: our hell is past, eighteen hundred years ago. His holy life is ours: our heaven was purchased *in Him*, by good works, centuries since. His purity of character is ours; now begun in us, and soon to be perfected there: " For we know that when He shall appear we shall be like Him." For He is now "made unto us wisdom, and righteousness, and sanctification, and redemption." In a word, it is thus that "he that hath the Son hath life."

" My beloved is mine, and I am His."

" And this is eternal life, that they might know thee, and Jesus Christ whom thou hast sent."

Upon this account comes the protection vouchsafed the Christian. Can disaster befall the glorified Son of God? How, then, can harm come to the disciple who is one with Him? "The sun shall not smite thee by day, nor the moon by night."

The poet Virgil gives a pleasing and suggestive fiction. He tells us how Venus, desiring to protect Æneas and his company, "so that no one might see them, stop them, or make them give account of their goings," threw around them a cloud of such peculiar texture that they were enabled to walk the streets of Carthage unseen and unmolested. This fiction becomes substantially a fact in the experience of every believer. For: —

"As the mountains are round about Jerusalem, so the Lord is round about His people from henceforth, even for ever."

"The Lord is my light and my salvation; whom shall I fear? The Lord is the strength of my life; of whom shall I be afraid?"

"The Lord is my Shepherd: I shall not want."

"I will lift up mine eyes to the hills from whence cometh my help. My help cometh from the Lord, which made heaven and earth."

"They that trust in the Lord shall be as Mount . Zion, which cannot be removed, but abideth for ever."

It is this sacred union, moreover, that underlies and gives force to the law, "Ask and ye shall receive." For the promise is: "If ye abide in me, and my words abide in you, ye shall ask what ye will and it shall be done unto you."

Can the hand need succor and the brain not know? or, knowing, shall it fail to devise help and healing? As quickly as the nerve-current carries the message of pain to the nerve-centre, does the uniting Spirit carry the soul's thrill and cry of distress to the Master. The union is perfect and complete. One needs but ask, to receive.

There is almost no limit to the resources thus placed in our hands: Christians may use them feebly and intermittently, or moderately and steadily, or largely and constantly. A few have dared "to take God at His word" and base their lives entirely on this divine law of supply and demand. George Müller is perhaps the most notable of these persons. They seem fanatical. Who shall say that they have exceeded the provisions of grace? At the least they have been sustained.

And there are many who, in the conduct of their ordinary business, endeavor to lay all their affairs before the Lord, and to act only upon His direction and with the means He puts in their hands.

In a word, " the secret of the Lord " inspires the soul to

PRAYER!

It is by prayer that the fruits of this secret become immediately available. There are other methods of contact, but prayer must vitalize them all, — even the reading of the Scriptures must be with prayer for the aid of the illuminating Spirit.

Were it possible that the believer should not pray and yet be a believer, he would still have this wealth at his command indeed, but it would lie unused until the Master should come, contract the elastic cord that binds them together, and present him perfected before the Father to enjoy in person the full fruits of redemption. This, in fact, is what happens in some degree to all, and almost entirely to many, because of the neglect of prayer. They are rich, yet they live like beggars! To whatever extent the neglect is permitted, so far these fruits are left to lie unused.

Many suppose that the law, " we are saved by hope, " is exclusive in the domain of Christian privilege; that all joy, all growth, all knowledge, are delayed until the hope shall reach full fruition at the Master's coming. There is, however, another law, the law of faith. We are saved by faith. Somewhat is indeed left to hope ; all the grandeur and glory of *manifestation* await its fulfilment. But *realization* attends faith. For: —

"Faith is the substance [realization*] of things hoped for, the evidence of things not seen."

* *Substance.* " It seems to me that the word here has reference to *something that imports reality,* in the view of the mind, to those things that are not seen . . . " BARNES.

And Paul says : —

" The life *I now live* in the flesh I live by the faith of the Son of God."

Now prayer is the appropriating act of faith. Prayer "realizes," brings to us the blessings we have now in store, whenever the occasion requires them, — as a man " realizes " on his stocks when he wants ready money. Prayer is a check on the bank, always honored. Our vast wealth lies there, in the person of the Son. We may draw upon these vast resources now, and daily. We may " realize " things unseen, and use them; yet still they remain unseen of men, save in their effects upon us and through us.

We may realize wisdom : " If any man lack wisdom, let him ask of God, who giveth to all men liberally and upbraideth not."

We may realize grace for every emergency : " My grace shall be sufficient for thee."

We may realize character. The riches of manhood in Christ are ours, and lie ready for our use. The feeblest may daily " grow in grace and the knowledge of our Lord and Saviour Jesus Christ " : —

" Till we all come, in the unity of the faith, and of the knowledge of the Son of God, unto a perfect man, unto the measure of the stature of the fulness of Christ. That we henceforth be no more children, tossed to and fro and carried about with every wind of doctrine. . . . But . . . may grow up into Him in all things which is the head, even Christ."

We may realize guidance, absolute and complete, minute and constant: " Commit thy way unto the Lord, . . . and He shall bring it to pass." " Thou shalt guide me with thy counsel."

We may realize peace : —

" Thou wilt keep him in perfect peace whose mind is stayed on Thee, because he trusteth in thee."

" Be careful for nothing ; but in every thing by prayer and supplication, with thanksgiving, let your requests be made known unto God ; and the peace of God, which passeth all understanding, shall keep your minds and hearts, through Christ Jesus."

" Peace I leave with you ; *My* peace I give unto you."

We may realize Christ's ineffable joy : —

"These things have I spoken unto you, that My joy might remain in you, and that your joy might be full."

"Ask, and ye shall receive, that your joy may be full."

Well, then, is it said : —

> "Prayer is the Christian's vital breath,
> The Christian's native air."

And well is it that we are so often and so urgently exhorted to pray : —

"Men ought always to pray, and not to faint."

"Pray without ceasing."

"In every thing . . . let your requests be made known unto God."

"Is any afflicted among you? let him pray."

It was not strange, since communion with Him is the secret of life, that after the turmoil and exhaustion of their preaching tour Christ said to his disciples, "Come ye yourselves apart [with Me] and rest awhile;" nor strange that Paul, before entering on the work of the Apostolate, was sent to spend three years in the silences of Arabia; nor yet that he preferred to "go afoot" from Troas to Assos while his ship sailed around the projecting land, that in the midst of his wearing work he might have a day in solitude with God.

Solitude is a relief to the Christian, — the working Christian ; rather than a burden, as to the world.

Let the Christian pray. Let him live in an atmosphere of prayer. Let him commune with God continually " of all that is in his heart." Let him acquire the habit of spreading all his affairs before the Lord, as Hezekiah disposed of Rabshakeh's letter.

There is nothing so minute or unimportant that God may not hear it. Whatever interests the soul interests the Master. Its pettiest trial, its pettiest pleasure, if pure, thrills to His sympathetic heart. The smallest interest is sacred in His kindly eyes.

" There is nothing that interests you that is too little to carry to your God in the solitude of closet prayer. You may enter into your chamber, shut your door, and, secure of a kindly hearing, you may tell your Father which is in secret, of little things that worry and vex you, which are yet so little that you would be ashamed to confess to your nearest friend how great a space they filled up in your heart. Fix it in your mind that there is no duty, however little, which we can do without God's help, and no temptation, however small, which we can resist without God's grace." *

There is something finely suggestive in the narrative concerning the disciples of John Baptist. Upon his death they "took up his body and buried it, — and went and told Jesus!"

The title of Anna Shipton's little book, "Tell Jesus," has a pleasing sound in the Christian's ear.

What shall not the soul tell Him? He welcomes the approach: —

"He waits to answer thee."

His warm heart yearns for the confidence of His child. He is pleased when the Christian breathes his little secrets in His ear. Tell Him all!

An American clergyman narrates the following incident: —

* Newspaper fragment from A. K. H. Boyd.

" The pastor of one of our Eastern churches was visiting London. He had met one of the merchants of the city in America, and had been urged to call upon him in case he should ever pass that way. Surmising that he must be very busy, and having but a few hours to spare, — and they in the very heart of the day, — he hesitated about intruding. Nothing but the memory of the urgent invitation prevented his omitting the call. Upon arriving he asked : —

" ' Can I see Mr. —— ? '

" ' No! he is very busy to-day. This is steamer day, and he cannot be interrupted by anybody.'

" ' Please take him my card.'

" In a moment Mr. —— appeared, his face lighted up with pleasure.

" ' Just as I expected Mr. ——; you are very busy. And now I will go away.'

" ' *No!* No!' was the response. ' Indeed you must come in.'

" Taking him into his office, without waiting to sit down, Mr. —— said : —

" 'I am very glad you have called. I would not have had you fail. I *am* very busy, but I always have a moment for my Lord. I have a little place here for private prayer. You must come in with me, and we shall have a season of prayer together.'

" They went into a small apartment, evidently set aside for this purpose.

" ' Now you lead in prayer.'

" It was done. Mr. —— followed. A hand-grasp followed beneath beaming countenances and moistened eyes; 'Good-bye' was hastily and warmly spoken; and the friends separated."

Only ten minutes for a friendship which spanned the ocean, and that claimed for prayer ! Their fellowship " of kindred minds," "like that above," drew them aside to commune with each other, first and only, by communing with the Master.

It is said on the same authority that several, perhaps many, merchants in one (and perhaps more) of our large cities, have fitted up for themselves dark, narrow, box-like closets,

8

whither, each by himself, they are wont to retire for a few minutes at times, during the pressure of the day's business, for the refreshment of soul, which they find they sadly need, in communion with God. One of these men is reported to have said: " On some days, if I had not that resort, I believe I should go mad! so great is the pressure."

In order, then, to the culture of brotherly love, to relief from burdens, to the supply of special wants, — spiritual or temporal, — to growth in grace; in fine, in order to the communication of the divine life to the soul, the realization in the present of the soul's wealth of resource in Christ, the enjoyment and profit of the secret of the Lord; — the soul should pray. Pray often. Pray ever.

" The secret of the Lord " is enjoyed through union with Christ, consummated and maintained by the Holy Spirit, — who animates the Scriptures as we read; who animates our returning prayer; through whom we commune with God, unseen of man, in the use of all the means of grace.

" Spirit of truth and grace,
    Come from above ;
Rest on us tenderly,
    Peace-speaking Dove.
Cherish our holy life ;
Banish our carnal strife,
    Fill us with love.

Show us Christ's lowly heart,
    Humble our pride ;
Bring us in penitence
    Close to His side.
Bring us around the Cross
Counting our gain but loss,
    There to ABIDE."

IV.

THE LAWS OF LIGHT.

"Whereunto we have already attained, let us walk by the same rule." — PHIL. iii. 16.

EVERY calling in life has its maxims, some of them false and unworthy, but all of them attempts at the crystallization of valuable experience for the guidance of the inexpert.

The disciple of truth, standing in the Light, will soon detect certain leading lines running through the whole domain. The knowledge of these lines will stand him in good stead in many a time of doubt. Where a specific direction is wanting, or seems wanting, for the guidance of conduct or of thought, an application of the principle involved will serve to supply the lack. There is an abundance of exact precept and doctrine in the Scriptures, but there are also these general laws, — sometimes formulated and expressed, sometimes lying just beneath the surface. These are to be used as guiding principles. Around them may crystallize a thousand opinions, and upon them may be based a thousand actions, for which no other direction may be at hand.

The Bible was designed to stimulate the human intellect to its utmost vigor. It does indeed descend to the level of the lowest: the smallest child beyond infancy, and the most chaotic mind above idiocy, may grasp the initial promise which guarantees salvation. But the Book does not *abide* on ground so low. It was given to draw men up. If the man stand still, his Bible leaves him. The Christian of sluggish and slothful intellect has practically but a minute fragment of a Bible. " Then shall we know *if we follow on to know* the Lord." The disciple should advance. He should soon begin "to put this and that together," to use his enfranchised reason with increasing discrimination in discovering and developing the seed-thoughts of truth. Let him become so much a MAN as to deduce and discern the laws of Light, and to apply them with a manly decision and discretion to the innumerable details of life. *Thus* shall the Light entirely guide his way.

1. *" Prove all things."*   A noted barrister instructing a student at law said: "First and always, take nothing for granted. Let there be proof of every thing." This is merely what the Scriptures command: " Prove all things : hold fast that which is good."

Any creed, party, sect, philosophy, scheme, which seeks the believer's countenance or co-operation, can have no claim upon him until he have himself proved its claim valid in the light of the Word. A fair seeming, a plausible pretence of righteousness and profit, will not suffice; nor even the quotation of a passage of Scripture which may seem to yield sanction to the thing proposed. The soul itself must take the matter up, bear it patiently into the full stream of Light, let rays fall upon it on this side and on that, and definitely ascertain its substantial accordance with the tenor of the law of God. If this accord cannot be made to appear, the Christian should not commit himself to it.

Nothing is to be done at random. The life is to be measured step by step; every step must be taken in the Light. The minutest affairs should not be left to regulate themselves, or to be regulated by the. mere impulse of the moment.

Decisions which from the nature of the case must be reached instantly, can be right only as they flow from an habitual compliance with the condition, "If ye abide in me, and my words abide in you . . . ." In such cases there is instantaneous direction. This, however, cannot be had except when it is needed: nor even then, unless the soul habitually abide in the Light. " Prove all things."

2. *Faith is the best sight :* "We walk by faith, not by sight." He who walks by sight, simply does as seems best: he merely guesses; he walks in darkness; for "there is no light in *him*." He who walks by faith does as God tells him: he does right; he walks in the Light. *So far* as he thus walk, he makes no mistake.

All things are part or product of God's thought. That thought, in its completeness, is too large for the grasp of the human understanding. Man has no line wherewith to measure God, nor any vessel large enough to contain a complete revelation of Him : the ocean cannot be put into a bucket. So God reveals only what we need to know. Man's knowledge, however derived, is in fragments : it cannot be framed into a complete and harmonious system. There will always be gaps, missing links ; and hence, mysteries.

The fragments of thought and fact which come to us, seem disjointed and ill-fitting. They do not therefore contradict each other. For instance, it is not in our power to harmonize man's suffering with God's love ; sin with Omnipotence ; free-will with Sovereignty. The missing links leave gaps. But these things are not contradictions ; they exist side by side as contradictions could not do.

Galileo declared the sphericity of the earth. The priests demanded : Why then do not men fall off from the under side? He could not answer: Newton had not yet formulated the law of gravitation. Was Galileo wrong? The very school-boy knows he was not. There was simply a missing link in the information at hand.

Men call this kind of thing a contradiction. It is not a contradiction. It is merely incongruity in our thought, resulting from the fragmentary state of our knowledge. Incongruity in our thought is not necessarily contradiction in fact: —

> " All discord — harmony not understood;
> All partial evil — universal good."

These are some of the problems which Nature suggests: there is more " mystery " in her realm than in that of Revelation. Nature lends no aid to their solution. What then?

We turn to the Light, — to God speaking through the Scriptures? Why? Because God knows: man only learns; and he had best learn from Him. Because God's testimony is the best testimony. If fragmentary, it yet is

8*   L

less so than that of our narrow observation, and
only as little so as the limitations of the human
mind require.   It is the best possible testimony
so far as it goes, and it goes further than any
other now afforded us.

He who walks by faith is guided by this
unerring, wide-shining Light.   His knowledge
is the largest, the most accurate, the most
satisfactory possible on earth.   Men otherwise
are but guessers at truth and duty, "ever
learning and never able to come to the knowledge of the truth," disagreeing among themselves, and each at different times with
himself.

It is this consideration which gives point to
the question, " Who art thou, O man, that re-
pliest against God?" and to God's demand of
Job: "Who is this that darkeneth counsel by
words without knowledge?"   Wisely did the
patriarch reply : —

"I know that thou canst do every thing, and that
no thought can be withholden from thee. *Who* is he
that darkeneth counsel by words without knowledge?

Therefore have *I* uttered that I understood not; things *too wonderful for me*, which I knew not ! "

Asaph was in doubt * while he thought men's thoughts, and the doubt brought pain : —

" When I thought to know this, it was too painful for me, until I went *into the sanctuary of God :* then understood I their end."

Faith is the best sight.   To receive what God says, to do what God requires, is the method of certainty and safety.   The sayings may seem incongruous, and the requirements may seem extravagant and impossible: but God knows; it is man's wisdom to acquiesce.

> " One part, one little part, we dimly scan
>   Through the dark medium of life's feverish gleam ;
> Yet dare arraign the whole stupendous plan,
>   If but that little part incongruous seem ;
> Nor is that part, perhaps, what mortals deem :
>   Oft from apparent ills our blessings rise.
> Ah ! then, renounce that impious self-esteem
>   That aims to trace the secrets of the skies ;
> For thou art but of dust !   Be humble, and be wise."

3. *The will of God is the sole arbiter of right.* God is the fountain of all existence, and, of

* Ps. lxxiii.

course, of all its laws. "Shall not the Judge of all the earth do right?" God can do no wrong, can require no wrong; else were He less than God. He can be trusted *out of sight!* He can be trusted to lay down the law for us.

Wherefore, in the last analysis, Right and Wrong split and divide upon His sovereign will. What God wills is right, is true, is best, — best for others and for us. Christ's climacteric characterization of His work was : —

"Lo, I come to do thy will, O God!"

"My meat is to do the will of Him that sent me!"

"I do always those things that please Him!"

This was His right-conduct, and He gives it as the ultimate law for ours. His prayer for Himself was : "Not my will, but thine, be done." And He taught us, as the sum and the crowning expression of our desire and prayer for both ourselves and others, to say : "Thy will be done on earth, as it is in heaven."

On this Will man may fall back, — for it is revealed for his guidance. Here he may stand, as on a rock which will not sink beneath him.

By this rule the conduct may be regulated, to this key the heart should be attuned. The whole life, including creed, character, and conduct, is to be conformed to God's will. To accomplish its dicta is the very loftiest aim of creature-life. It was the avowed aim of Jesus' life: who shall dare the attempt to excel Him!

4. *The creature belongs to the Creator.*

" Behold, all souls are mine ! "

" Shall the thing formed say to Him that formed it, Why hast thou made me thus ? "

Wherefore the law is given : —

" Fear God and keep His commandments, for this is the whole duty of man ! "

" Whether therefore ye eat, or drink, or whatsoever ye do, do all to the glory of God ! "

The manufacturer and the inventor have prior claim upon the product of their genius, their skill, their time, toil, and means. Much more has God the supreme claim on man. Had there been no redemption, man still would have belonged, and apart from redemption man still does belong, to God. His time, talent, means, influence, person; all that he has and all that he is, — are God's. "Man's chief end is to glorify God, and to enjoy Him for ever." *

5. *The redeemed belong to the Redeemer.* Wherefore, God only could redeem; if for no other reason, lest there be a conflict of claim.

"Ye are not your own; ye are bought with a price; therefore glorify God in your body and spirit, which are God's."

"Ye are bought with a price; be not ye the servants of men."

"Forasmuch as ye know that ye were not redeemed with corruptible things, as silver and gold, . . . but with the precious blood of Christ."

It is then most natural that Christ, on His departure, should leave with His disciples the command, "Occupy till I come." It is natural that He should claim all our time, our thought, our toil. It belongs to Him. Our business belongs to Him: it should be conducted solely in His interests. Our recreations belong to Him. Our petty savings, or our wealth, nay our daily

* Westminster Shorter Catechism.

earnings even, are His! to be distributed (or held) as He may indicate.

6. *The claims of men follow the claims of God.* God is first; the divine fatherhood must of necessity be, before any human brotherhood become possible. The first table of the moral law has the precedence. To know, worship, revere, and obey God are obligations which underlie all others. To neglect one of these things is a greater crime than theft or murder, other conditions in the case being equal. No one guilty of this neglect has any just claim to the appellation "a moral man."

"The first and greatest commandment is, Thou shalt love the Lord thy God with all thy heart, with all thy soul, with all thy mind, and with all thy strength."

He who ignores this law and these claims, gives no guarantee that he will regard those which are minor and dependent, — those which forbid murder, adultery, theft, slander. In their interior sense, "love," he *cannot* obey them except he first love God. He may be

trusted to regard even their external requirements, only so far as it may be convenient for
him to do so; only so far as habit of thought
and action, self-respect, fear of civil law, and
the like, may compel him. He who ignores the
Father is apt to end by ignoring the brother.
The greater before the less. The foundation
before the superstructure. The root before the
branch. The claims of men cannot precede or
rival the claims of God.

But they do follow : —

" And the second commandment is like unto it,
Thou shalt love thy neighbor as thyself."

The six laws of human relationship immediately follow the four which regulate duty to
God. There is no omission. The duty is made
plain. Man is a debtor to his neighbor: " For
no man liveth to himself, and no man dieth to
himself." Each man is part of a vast framework ; every other man is in some sense his
neighbor. The weakest has some influence,
some " opportunity," that touches all the rest.
We are inextricably bound up together. Dis-

order in one part, thrills through the structure. Righteousness in the humblest man, reaches the eyes of others and serves both God and man. Every act gives out its influence. Every moment is freighted with responsibility.

" Each man has some part to play ! "

And law governs the whole. Man in relations with man, as with God, is not free from the direction of law, from the obligations of duty, for a single moment.

7. *Form follows fact.* Redemption was a fact before it was given form on Calvary. Revelation was a fact before it was filled to completeness and crystallized into shape in Scripture. The soul is before the body. The covenant is before baptism. Faith precedes fidelity. The inner life must precede the conduct.

God's method is " from within outward," not from without inward. The tree is developed from within the seed. Righteousness is developed from within the heart. Salvation must be wrought in before it can be " worked out: "

"Work *out* your own salvation with fear and trembling, for it is God that worketh *in* you both to will and to do of His good pleasure."

That is, the form should follow. What is in the heart should be displayed in the speech and conduct. The assertion, " The light . . . hath shined in our hearts," meets the quick response, " Let your light so *shine!*" The life should " bring forth fruit." Faith should issue in confession of faith, in good works. Love begins by loving, and expends itself in serving.

So, also, the church invisible seeks visible expression, — so long as God makes Christians, Christians *will* have " churches." Thought seeks utterance by word; the thought of God, by the sermon, the address, the word of counsel, the publication. The Christian's knowledge tends to crystallize in dogmas; the summary of Christian faith, in creeds. And as long as Christians continue to learn, we shall, with equal Scriptural warrant for their *right* use, have sermons and books, dogmas and creeds. Every preacher, not a fool, dogmatizes; nor can he avoid doing so. Every intelligent Christian has his creed, partial or complete, unwritten or expressed: there is a necessity in the very nature of the case. The modern railing at creeds and dogmas is but the din of folly: wise men who join in it *intend* only to rebuke the unwarranted use so often made of them.

Forms are not to be slighted or neglected because the facts take precedence. Form and fact are inseparable. The formless is useless — for man. Man knows even God, only as He takes form, reveals Himself. Forms have their place, and impose on us the necessity of using them. The Bible, the Church, the Sabbath, Baptism and the Supper, the formal confession of Christ, the vocal prayer and praise, all have valid claims. There can be no rightful neglect of them, even upon plea of superlative spirituality. Any neglect is *prima facie* evidence that the spiritual life is either wanting or waning. If the soul were emancipated from *its* " form," the body, then might the warranted forms of Christianity be laid aside ; not otherwise. Death comes, in-

deed ; but also the resurrection ; and the soul's
need of form persists unto this last cry: "Not
for that we would be unclothed, but clothed
upon."

8. " *The letter killeth, but the spirit giveth life.*"
Human words and forms express God's facts
only approximately, not accurately. The facts
are too large; forms of speech, of service, of
conduct, are not adequate to hold them. They
overflow, like a river that has burst its banks:
in certain exigencies the channel proves too
narrow and too shallow for the stream. There
is sometimes an overflow of the best literal rule,
— even one given by God, if encased in human
language. There is a superabundance of wealth
in Christ which no words can fully suggest.
There is a breadth in the responsibilities of life,
in the government of God, in the possibilities
of redeemed manhood, which sometimes over-
spreads all bounds of language or rule.

Christ sacrificed literal accuracy by quoting
from the Septuagint, the common version of the
time, rather than make His words less profitable

by the use of the exact Hebrew. " The Sabbath was made for man, and not man for the Sabbath." Christ himself baptized not, but His disciples ; and Paul said, " I thank God I baptized none of you save Crispus and Gaius. . . . For Christ sent me not to baptize, but to preach the gospel." The law, even of the Sabbath or of Baptism, may meet an emergency for which its letter does not provide.

It is not always safe to press every point, every analogy, of a parable to a doctrinal or practical conclusion. The leading idea of the teaching must rule, not the aggregation of minute suggestions ; the spirit, not the letter.

" Form follows fact," and may vary in aspect or in method for the sake of preserving the " fact " uninjured. The Lord's Supper is not observed by anybody in a reclining posture, and rarely by night or in an upper room ; yet the observance is lawful and sufficient.

No typical sacrifice, ordinance, character, or structure conveyed the full idea of Christ which it suggested, or failed to present points in which no analogy could be traced. " The law " gave but a shadow of good things to come, and by development the revelation of Redemption outgrew it: " The law was given by Moses, but grace and truth came by Jesus Christ." The river burst its banks : Judaism perished.

The Sermon on the Mount gave an early, a complete, and a standing rebuke to the exaggeration of " the letter " at the expense of " the spirit." Yet the letter is binding, in its order. The vessel should be carefully kept and carried, lest the precious contents be spilled. The contents can be preserved and used, only by the employment, not the neglect, of the vessel which contains them. Grace is to be had only by the careful, patient, almost reverential keeping and use of the means, the agencies, the forms, the rules, through which it is conveyed.

A vessel may, however, by careless use, become dented, defaced ; yet the contents are not destroyed, nor usually vitiated. The Bible was copied, translated ; man's finger-marks are on it : yet it is the Bible still, the adequate and authoritative revelation of God in Christ. Customs and rules, even forms imposed by Scripture, may undergo changes. Suppose the change in any given case be for the worse: grace still flows through. Those who have made the change need not be unchurched or called apostate.

And again: while a curb and windlass may be needed at a well, the curb should not be built so high, nor the windlass made so heavy, that the little child or a feeble man may not obtain water in his thirst!

9. *God works by processes,* not by a series of isolated efforts. His law of grace is, growth.

The Bible grew, and was sixteen centuries in reaching completeness. The Sabbath was more than four thousand years in attaining its present grandeur. The idea of Redemption, as a revelation, dates from the fall, and received its latest development one hundred years after Christ was born. The visible church is a growth whose germs lie far back in the ages.

The Christian grows, as a child. He needs

nourishment and exercise. He may be over-
taxed. He needs patient waiting and tender
cherishing. His first judgments are crude and
inaccurate. His early ideas are vague and partial, as an infant's.*

The individual church grows, both outward
and upward, by a process which seems painfully
tedious. The prevalence of righteousness in
the land, in the world, in realms of trade, law,
society, is a matter of slow growth. And the
in-gathering of the great host of the redeemed is
an achievement to which God lends the meas-
ureless power of *Time.* For the law is : —

" Precept *must be* upon precept, precept *upon* precept ; line upon line, line upon line ; here a little and
there a little."

10. *Obligations never conflict;* they come in
order.

The various institutions and relations in life,
are recognized in the Word. God, one's own
soul, the family, the vocation, the church, Society, and the State, have their several claims.

* *See* Eph. iv. 10–16.

There is room even for other institutions, — industrial associations, charitable organizations, voluntary societies. The Light shines on all the relationships of life. The order of obligation may vary with the individual and the time, but the various obligations can never come in conflict; there is always a preference, and each one may, at the time, ascertain what it is.

"To obey the powers that be," to walk "among men," to be "diligent in business," to rule and cherish one's own household, to regard "the assembling of yourselves together," to lend a helping hand to a neighbor; these things are duties as well as to "watch and pray" and to "worship God."

True life is broad, includes all the elements of righteousness, shirks nothing, puts all in order, so as to make the best use of all for the glory of God.

11. *Little things are the great things.*

"Despise not the day of small things."

"Here a little, and there a little."

9　　　　　M

" He that is faithful in that which is least is faithful also in much; and he that is unjust in the least . . . "

" Whosoever shall give to drink unto one of these little ones, a cup of cold water only . . ."

" And Jesus called a little child unto Him, and set him in the midst of them, and said, Except ye . . . become as little children . . ."

" Whosoever . . . shall humble himself as this little child, the same is greatest . . ."

" And whoso shall receive one such little child in my name, receiveth ME. But whoso shall offend one of these little ones that believe in me, it were better for him . . ."

" Suffer the little children and forbid them not to come unto me, for of such is the kingdom of heaven."

" Fear not, little flock, for it is your Father's good pleasure to give *you* the kingdom."

" Inasmuch as ye have done it unto one of the least of these my brethren, ye have done it unto me."

" Take us the foxes, the little foxes, that spoil the vines."

" A little more slumber, a little more sleep, . . . *so* shall thy poverty come . . ."

" Then he that had the one talent came, and said . . ."

This law of the value of littles is something marvellous in its way. It seems to obtain everywhere. One is safe in applying it in any direction. The most paradoxical form of stating it seems the most nearly accurate.

This is altogether in contrast with the notions of men. Men look for and worship large things. There are few " big things " in Grace; " not much " is its law; its greatness, its surpassing grandeur, are brought about by littles. The vast sweep of Providence is accomplished by the painstaking care of the sparrows, of the hairs of one's head, of the lot " cast into the lap," of the tear-drop on an infant Moses' cheek. Redemption has its glory in its comprehension of many minute events, both in its purchase and in its application.

Man must be content to be " a little one," a " babe " in Christ at first, — a weak and it may be wayward Christian; he may not wait to make his start, expecting to be wise and well-grown from the outset. If any Christian seem sturdy from the beginning, either there is a delusive appearance, or his spiritual vigor has its root in a slow and careful former training.

Growth in the knowledge of the Scriptures, comes only by patient use of littles. All good habits are formed by littles. All great ingatherings result from former work in littles. Little sins are the most dangerous. Little trials are the most grievous; a quaint writer has told us that it is not the great stones in the way that most distress the traveller, but the little pebbles, which cut the feet.

The claims of the children — upon the family, the community, and the church — *are prior to and stronger than those of adults.* Our prayers, expenditures, and labors should ever yield their needs the precedence. This fact, so plainly taught, seems to be but crudely apprehended as yet, even by the church!

It is the little things God is pleased to have us tell Him. Our little joys make up far the greater part of our happiness. Little duties make up the most of life. The work of our one-talent Christians is more needed by the cause of Christ to-day, than all that abler and wealthier men could do.

In a word, the little things are everywhere the essential things. Without them, the great results had not been achieved; nor can others be brought about, save by their aggregation.

On this subject God demands a complete revolution of the world's ideas. That the revolution is needed, shows how viciously the human intellect is warped by sin. Redemption will not be complete, until a prime and painstaking regard for the little things be substituted for the amazing disregard of them even now prevalent.

12. *Death is in order to life.*

" Except a corn of wheat fall into the ground and die, it abideth alone ; but if it die, it bringeth forth much fruit."

Christ must needs die in order to redeem men : " If He shall make his soul an offering for sin . . ." is the condition of the covenant.

Each economy of grace dies, that from its decay may spring the growing germ of one larger and grander, as the Jewish economy died to make way for the present dispensation. The carnal heart dies by reason of the begetting of a new life within. The body dies; and from its germ, Christ present with it, there shall proceed the more glorious body of the resurrection. The heavens and the earth that now are, shall pass away; and from their ruins shall appear "a new heaven and a new earth, wherein dwelleth righteousness." The race of man died in sin; then began the development, from their number, of the new and more glorious race of the redeemed, begotten of "the second Adam, the Lord from heaven." Old habits and loves must die when one, in Christ, becomes "a new creature;" and new habits and affections develop, some of them (as parental love) akin to the old in name, but new in fact and far more worthy. The Christian is dead; nevertheless, he lives; yet not he, but Christ liveth in him; and the new life is glorious beyond the conception even of its possessor.

There is a relation. The germ ever feeds upon the decaying matter of the seed. Redemption feeds upon Christ's "body and blood." The gospel dispensation fed, even now feeds, upon the Mosaic. The Christian feeds upon the better habits, the worldly education and prestige, of his former life. The rule is constant.

13. *Peace comes by war.* Christ said, "I came not to bring peace, but a sword." The truth must fight its way. The Gospel provokes men; it must rise, as it has ever risen, against wind and tide.

"This world was made for climbing on."

One makes headway only through struggles. All good work is hard work. Especially does the best work, Christian labor, call for both toil and pain. The Christian has constant "fightings within." As Christ must suffer in order to save; as the soul is in the pangs of conviction before it is born to joy in Christ; so the Christian must bear the cross before he wear the crown: "*If we suffer* with Him, we shall be also glorified together." Christians are enjoined to "put on the whole armor of God" and to "take the sword of the Spirit, which is the word of God."

All truth hurts. We must expect opposition.

"Cursed are ye when all men speak well of you." It will not do to court popular favor. Preaching to suit the times, is not apt to be preaching Christ. Creeds most fought against, are likely to prove the nearest true. The sermon that cuts deepest, will probably do the most good. Anger is a good sign; indifference, even negative pleasure, is to be feared; these indicate freezing to death! Christians reel and stagger under the doctrines they most need to hear: the weak eye smarts in the strong light. The cry for smooth things from the oracles of God, and the healing of the hurt of men slightly, saying, " Peace, peace, when there is no peace," are evils explicitly and repeatedly denounced in the Scriptures. Sin must be conquered! War must come in order to peace. " The word of God is sharper than any two-edged sword, piercing to the dividing asunder of soul and spirit, . . . and is a discerner of the thoughts and intents of the heart." Cut deep!

14. *Self-sacrifice is success;* the only success. The noblest life is living for others. The

greatest happiness is found by ignoring it as an end, and living for God.

" Whosoever will save his life, shall lose it; and whosoever will lose his life for my sake, shall find it."

God's constant thought is for His creation, not for Himself; hence His matchless glory. His revelation of Himself in Christ displays the most exhaustive and exhausting self-sacrifice, both as the right method of action and the true method of success: " Ought not Christ to have suffered, and to enter into His glory."

Our rights are best maintained by ignoring them; if insisted on and asserted, it should be only for the sake of others, not of self. True nobility lies in thoughtlessness of self : —

" Look not every man on his own things; but every man also on the things of others."

" We then that are strong ought to bear the infirmities of the weak, and not to please ourselves. Let every one of us please his neighbor. . . . For even Christ pleased not Himself."

True manhood is in serving others. The great Example is one of utter self-sacrifice; and it

9*

compels men's admiration and wins men's hearts! "The good Shepherd giveth His life for the sheep."

This self-sacrifice is not to be intermittent, or only occasional. It is the *law* of life. Christ said: "I do always those things that please Him."

15. *Service is ennobling.* Perhaps at no point do we see more plainly than here that God's thoughts are not as men's thoughts, nor His ways as theirs. But God is right: men are mistaken. The law which affirms the nobility of service gives the flat contradiction to the assumptions of men, and the rebuke direct to their most ineradicable feelings and actions.

Paul boasted himself a slave of Jesus Christ. Our Lord made himself a servant to us. His filling the place of the lowest menial when washing the disciples' feet, was in immediate * rebuke of the strife "which should be greatest."

"He that will be greatest among you, let him be least of all, and servant of all."

* *Compare* Luke xxii. 24–27 *with* John xiii. 1–16.

The only true exaltation is through the most devoted service. The Master has honored and hallowed the title " servant," beyond the power of men to fix opprobrium upon it.

16. *The most binding servitude is the truest freedom.* There is no servitude so lasting, so manifold in its chains, so intense in its devotion, as servitude to Christ; and none other is so free as His servant. Paul, boasting himself Christ's slave, yet exulted in the freedom of a son in the same house with Him. The promise is, " . . . the truth shall make you free ; " yet this freedom is only unto the service of righteousness : " But now, being made free from sin, and become servants to God . . . "

Sin pays wages, — "death ; but the gift of God is eternal life ; " and the gift binds in a stronger devotion than the wages. Gratitude brings the most faithful servitude, and this servitude is the truest freedom. The more the Christian loves his Lord, the more *free* he feels to *serve* Him ; the less he loves, the more is his service hampered and constrained.

Freedom from Christ is slavery to sin. This servitude is unsatisfactory at best: it galls and frets. God breaks it: a new service begins, — the service of Christ. This bondage can never be broken! It is, freely, everlasting; no release can be given, none is sought. The more the Christian sees of this service, the more he loves it; he is more free unto it, the more he is bound; and the more Love binds him to it, the more free he becomes in rendering it, and the more he rejoices in it and seeks its enlargement. The more he realizes that he is saved, freed from the obligation of fear, the more does love grow and the larger is his labor. The silken cord is stronger than the iron chain.

The less the Christian supposes Christ has done for Him, the less is the sense of his obligation: his service seems more compulsory, seems mere hard duty; wherefore the less is rendered, and the more irksome it is. The greater is the sense of obligation because of a larger vision of Christ's gifts, the greater also is the willingness of proffer and rendition, and the more fully is it realized that the "yoke is easy," and "the burden light."

The freedom of the haughty soul to think for itself, ignoring the Scriptures, is slavery to ignorance and prejudice. The greater the restriction to the Word as the source of light, the greater is the freedom to knowledge, the more readily it is obtained, and the more satisfactory it seems.

Similarly, the greater the certainty of events because of God's sovereignty, the more firmly is free agency established. The more minute and complete God's rule, even in the heart, the more man also has "his own way." Everywhere, "the most binding servitude is the truest freedom."

17. *Love is law.* Men deem love and law in conflict. As usual, men err. Love is law; gives law; is the spirit vitalizing all good law; "is the fulfilling of the law." "God so loved the world . . . " Even hell is a fruit of love. The eternal punishment of the wicked *in* hell pro-

ceeds from love, even from love to them. " God *is* love."

Man cannot obey, save by loving: Christ's love is the mainspring of our love, whence proceeds our service. Fear may have fruit; hate is strong; self-respect may lead men far; conscience also operates; but love is the only *constraining* motive : " The love of Christ constraineth us ," said Paul. God reconstructs men on the principle of love. " Love is law."

18. *Weakness is strength.* Self-confidence, in the ordinary sense of the term, is an injury; self-distrust, a help. " Put no confidence in the flesh." The antiphony is, " Rejoice in Christ Jesus." To the Christian, self is nothing ; Christ, every thing. Trusting in self is leaning on a bruised reed: it will break and thrust one through. Our salvation is Christ, not some grace or gift imparted by Christ and separated from Himself. Our resources are not in self, but in Him. The sense of weakness is not a nerveless, useless hand, but an index-finger pointing the soul to its true Resort:

" When I am weak, then am I strong." Why? Because, " I can do all things through Christ which strengtheneth me." "Is any thing too hard for the Lord ? "

Only when one finds he is lost, does he desire Christ. The deeper the sense of need, the speedier and more sure is the flight to safety, and the more unreserved the trust.

The sense of guilt, of indwelling sin, of inherent weakness, cannot be too deep. The ruin, the helplessness, even the inability of the soul, cannot be made too plain. Job came at last to " abhor " himself; *then* he found his lost joy — in God. The deeper the knowledge of sin, the greater is the appreciation of salvation, and the larger are the gratitude, the joy, the eagerness to serve. Despair of self brings hope : self-hope is ruin.

The more one wants Christ, the more quickly he finds Him ; the more he wants *in* Christ, the more he finds in Him ; the more *of* Christ he wants, the more he receives.

The sinner's strength is to do nothing, but to

trust in what Christ has done. The Christian's strength is to *be* nothing, and to find Christ his All in All. The worker's strength is to be weak, and to call to his aid the infinite resources of his Lord.

To say, " I cannot," though it be true, does not free from the obligation nor make the service an impossibility. One can do whatever God wants him to do, though it were to remove mountains; by knowing that he can do nothing, and that Christ in him can do all things.

19. *The pilgrim is the best citizen.* He who feels least at home on earth, has the deepest interest in the welfare of men, — even their present welfare. He who has "no continuing city" here, seeking "one to come," is best prepared to administer the affairs of the city here. He who has least interest in earth, has the best interest.

It is a great mistake to suppose that longing for heaven unfits for contentment, even repose, on earth. The man who most wants to be there, is most content here : the best Christian has, of all men, the least tendency to suicide. The more he realizes the life to come, the more he makes of the life that now is. The more ready he is to depart, the more willing is he to stay.

Companionship with Christ, fits for the best companionship with men. He who, from principle, makes most light of earthly disaster, is most studious to avoid it. The more absorbed the soul becomes in Christ, the broader becomes its thought and the more tender its care, for men. The more one anticipates and realizes his citizenship in heaven, the more careful is he to be a good citizen on earth. The more he grows absorbed in Christ's kingdom, the more faithful and judicious he becomes in the affairs of his own government.

The more he rejoices in his home in heaven, the sweeter becomes his earthly home: he makes it better; he loves it more. The more he condemns sin, the more he loves the sinner. The more he aspires for himself, the lower he stoops to save others. As he becomes purer, he becomes more charitable in his judgments of his

N

fellows. In a word: the better fitted he becomes to enter upon the fruition of his heavenly citizenship, the more peaceable, helpful, open-handed citizen of earth he is.

No more grave error is committed than that which imputes to the Christian the loss of interest in, or of fitness for, earthly pursuits. On the contrary, the more intently he follows the pursuits of his high calling, the more interested, prudent, faithful, and successful he comes to be in all the proper pursuits of earth ; *for those include these.* — Take the cases of Joseph and Daniel. — The more a man is "a pilgrim and a stranger here," the more is he the best citizen, the most stable man in every respect.

These are a few of the Laws of Light. The Scriptures present many others. They are to be discerned by vigilant use of the vision, standing in the Light. They are designed to stimulate independent (yet divinely guided, and so safe and accurate) thought, back toward the origin of things, and forward toward various applications of them in practical matters of opinion and action. Thus the Christian may come to walk in the Light with some ease and freedom; he may be able to say with David : —

> " And I will walk at liberty,
> For I seek thy precepts."

PART FOURTH.

—◆—

WALKING IN THE LIGHT.

(Christian Conduct.)

———

" Walk as children of Light."—Eph. v. 8.

" His wisdom ever waketh,
　His sight is never dim ;
　He knows the way He taketh,
　And I will walk *in Him !* "

I.

WHAT? AND WHY?

"Let your light so shine before men . . ." — MATT. v. 16.

"HE is active in the church, but he is a *leetle* sharp in a trade."

This remark was passed in comment on the character and conduct of a professing Christian. Although calmly made and not meant in bitterness, it produced a puncture; for it was true, when it ought not to have been true, and it was unwittingly based on a logical distinction and a just preference.

There is a distinction between conduct and labor; and in the Christian life the realm of conduct has the preference, both in the order of time and in the order of importance.

To *be* right is of course the first thing : character precedes even conduct. To do right in the common affairs of life, comes next. Here is a broader field for righteousness, a field more pressing in its claims, than that of special and occasional effort.

The command " Walk in the Light," as used in the Scriptures, ordinarily refers to the Christian's demeanor in the common ways of life. It has, of course, its subjective aspect, looking to his thoughts, opinions, comforts. To these things extended reference has been made.* The bulk of thought designed to be suggested by the phrase seems, however, to regard the objective aspect, the appearance, the daily speech and conduct: " Walk circumspectly, redeeming the time ; " " walk honestly ; " " walk not as other Gentiles walk ; " " walk after His commandments."

This phase of the Christian life takes precedence of all that is signified by the terms, " zeal," " activity," " effort," " working for Christ."

" He that saith he is in the Light, and hateth his brother, is in darkness until now."

" If a man say he love God, and hateth his brother, he is a liar."

* *See* Part Third : " Standing in the Light."

He who is in the habit of saying these things,
takes on the form of Christian zeal. He becomes a sort of evangelist. He is " active."
He " speaks for Christ." He rises often in the
prayer-meeting, in the class-meeting, in the convention. Yet in the cases to which reference
is made, his conduct belies his words. So his
" saying," his " testimony for Christ," goes for
nothing. He has omitted the important thing.
The first and great fruit is lacking: it must
therefore be that the root is not in him; hence,
the gaudy appearance of the more showy fruit
is a mockery. His good works are

> "A painted ship upon a painted ocean."

His zeal is factitious. " He is a liar."

" In this the children of God are manifest . . . ;
whosoever doeth not righteousness is not of God, neither he that hateth his brother."

" He that saith he abideth in Him ought also so to
walk, even as He walked."

> " So let our lips and lives express
> The holy Gospel we profess ;
> So let our walk and conduct shine,
> To prove the doctrine all divine."

10

This matter of the Christian's ordinary conduct, is made the theme of a host of urgent and varied exhortations, injunctions, and warnings, from the lips of Jesus and the apostles. Only afterward and subordinately, is special service enjoined. He who neglects this order, who makes church matters and evangelistic work his prime care, to the neglect and injury of his common conduct, who forgets that Christ is glorified more by Christ-likeness in every-day affairs than by perfervid utterances and aggressive zeal, — places himself in the same category with those whom the Master thus addressed : —

"Wo unto you, scribes and Pharisees, hypocrites ! for ye pay tithe of mint, anise, and cummin, and have omitted the weightier matters of the law, — judgment, mercy, and faith. These ought ye to have done, and not to leave the others undone."

Each of these things is binding, but each in its order. *First*, the conduct.

" Let your light so shine before men, that they may see your good works, and glorify your Father . . ."

" For the grace of God . . . hath appeared, . . . teaching us that denying ungodliness we should live soberly, righteously . . ."

" Let your conversation be as it becometh the gospel of Christ."

" This is love, that we walk after His commandments."

" Walk in the way of good men."

The full statement of this duty is, Christ-likeness. To do, to speak, to be silent, to suffer, as Christ would do ; to manifest at every point the Spirit of Christ that is in us ; to do nothing from a worldly motive or in a worldly manner, but all for Jesus' sake, and in the way that will best please Him ; to display unostentatiously, quietly, constantly, *naturally* and not by pressure, the fruit which shall prove the presence of Christ in us, — this is walking in Light. And to the undertaking and maintenance of just this walk, every Christian is urgently, repeatedly, persistently called.

This is honest. Thus shall we be seen as we are. Who would sail under false colors?

Imagine the Hartford hoisting the black flag of piracy!

What is the Christian? A *Christian!* He is dead, and Christ liveth in him. This new life is his choice. The "body of death" still clings to him, but this is his shame and sorrow. Let the disgrace be kept hid. "I keep my body under." Let the true life appear. "By their fruits shall ye know *them.*"

This is profitable for men. It reaches them in the name of Christ, and touches them where they are most tender and most accessible.

Mr. J—— and Mr. R——, both infidels, one of them a violent and dissolute man, became Christians at length. Through what agency? Not church-effort: they scorned churches. Not by evangelistic address: they hooted at it. Their conversion was the fruit of the godly, patient, silent lives of two devoted Christian women. The wife of one dared not speak, had she chosen. Both women thought it best not to speak. They suffered; they prayed — and waited. After many a weary year, their waiting was crowned with manifest success. The steady stream of silent influence could not be stopped, it could not be met by abuse, and it could not be resisted.

This is pleasing to God. He is well pleased with such sacrifice. This " is more than all whole burnt-offerings and sacrifices." Nothing pleases God so much as likeness to Himself.

This is pre-eminently honoring to Christ. The so-called "moral" life, with no Christ in it, does not fall in this category. But the life which avowedly derives its supplies from Christ, and which proves by its common and constant fruit that these supplies are real and rich, is greatly to His honor. Men may not always be converted by it; but they know whom to credit, and the credit is duly given, — often openly. Although like Julian the Apostate they may reject Christ to the last, yet like him they will say : "*Galilean, thou hast conquered!* " Thus men shall know that " their rock is not as our Rock, even our enemies themselves being judges."

"If ye love me, keep my commandments."

"Ye are a chosen generation, a royal priesthood, a holy nation, a peculiar people; that ye should show forth the praises of Him who hath called you into His marvellous *Light.*"

II.

IN THE HOME.

" God setteth the solitary in families." — Ps. lxviii. 6.

THE family relation is an institution of God. It lies at the root of all human development, thrift, enjoyment. It is the normal unit of society, of the state, of the church. These three make up the vast framework of human life: this one is the foundation of the whole. The family is the seed from whose germ all healthy growth develops, — growth national, social, ecclesiastical: there are apparent exceptions, but they vanish under analysis.

God declares himself to be the " God of all the families of Israel." He promises blessings to "the seed of the righteous." Observation shows that blessings are apt to descend from parent to child. " Heredity" has its root in the Bible! Inheritance is a law of the state.

Parentage gives the place in society. The family is the true unit.

" Come thou and all thy house into the ark, for *thee* have I found faithful."

" The promise is unto you and to your children."

" The unbelieving husband is sanctified by the wife, and the unbelieving wife by the husband; else were your children unclean; but now are they holy."

The family relationship finds its symmetry and completeness, only in the Home. The family is the soul, the home is the breathing body which it animates. The family is the fact which seeks expression in the home as the form of its existence, the method of its development, and the agency of its influence.

The Home is an ordinance of God. It is the very fundamental ordinance, as is suggested by its nature, which observation discloses; by its origin, which history reveals; and by its place and function, which the Scriptures teach.

" And the Lord God took the man, and put him into the garden of Eden. . . . "

" Every wise woman buildeth her house."

" He blesseth the habitation of the just."

Many people have no home. This is not in accordance with the design of God. The life attains its best development and wields its best influence, when the home is its pivot and centre. The family life is dwarfed, it pines and eventually dies, if persistently denied the protecting and cherishing influences of the home. Life in a boarding-house or at a hotel, is not favorable to the development of the highest type of piety. Jesus saw fit, houseless and homeless as He was in the fulness of His privation as Redeemer, to *make* a home for a season at Peter's house in Capernaum, and to enter into the home-life of the family in Bethany.

Our young men and women are often too eager to relinquish their homes, not usually for others, in marriage, but for an Arab life. Jesus remained in His mother's house until He was thirty years of age. Yet his life-work ended at thirty-three!

Too many from unworthy motives shrink from and delay, or refuse marriage. Very

10*   o

often this is at the mere behests of worldly fashion : until they can have a fashionable home, they will have none. Jesus saw fit to perform His first miracle at a feast given in honor of the marriage of a poor couple.

The same folly frequently obtains in the formation of the relation. The choice is not seldom lightly made, made hastily, thoughtlessly, regardless of just requirements, and in obedience to a foolish taste, a headlong passion, or a wicked ambition. Abraham's care in providing for his son Isaac, is worth remembering ; and upon Solomon's folly in seeking an Egyptian alliance, History rings out a warning which echoes still.

Having the home, many yield readily to the temptation to sacrifice its claims to the clamors of the vocation. The demands of the counting-room, the office, or the farm, are permitted to absorb so much attention that the home is wickedly robbed.

Duty begins in the home. It is a mistake to suppose that even the church has a prior claim.

As a rule, the precedence is to be given to the advantages, the opportunities, the necessities, the religious culture, the happiness, of one's own household. If the rule must sometimes yield, the necessity should be regarded in the light of a calamity, and no stress of circumstances should suffice to make the calamity the rule; this "injunction" ought never to be made "perpetual."

The Christian should manifest a Christ-like spirit at home. The common virtues should be cultivated and displayed here above all other places. Meekness, patience, cheerfulness, *constant* self-sacrifice, a rigid truthfulness, sympathy, love; there is vast need of these things in our Christian homes, and a vast lack of them! Nowhere else will these virtues accomplish so much, nowhere else will their absence prove so mischievous. In the tender and close relations of the family, the least disorder will cause a jar. The machinery of home requires much oil to prevent friction. Its sensitive harmony is easily put out of tune.

Fretting; grumbling; constant or frequent fault-finding; the appropriation of the best things; thoughtlessness of the others; a gloomy. countenance; sharp, cutting words; deceptions; suspicions; alienations; exactions; undue restrictions; cheerlessness; the maintenance of a sullen or morbid silence; the banishment of generous laughter and all the lighter pleasures, or even the neglect to provide and stimulate these pleasures,—these are some of the ills by which many a Paradise is marred, and many a one destroyed. Incalculable harm is done. Christ is dishonored.

The Christian father who habitually comes home at evening too late to greet the children, or so worried and worn that he will not unbend or relax; the Christian mother and wife who prefers fashionable society or neighborhood gossip to the task of setting and keeping her house in order, and impressing the Master's spirit upon it; the Christian young man who treats his home as if it were a boarding-house; and the Christian young woman who makes it a

mere kingdom of convenience, — these are mur-
derers of home-life.

The smile, the cheerful greeting morning and
evening, the word tenderly spoken, the thoughtful act of kindness, are little things, cheap and
full of good fruit. It is no small task to so
persist in this conduct, to cultivate the spirit of
the Master to such an extent, that these fruits
of righteousness shall *characterize* the household; yet this is precisely what is required.

Further: The Christian should, to the extent
of his influence and authority, introduce and
maintain the worship of God in the home.
Godliness is even before brotherly kindness.
The ordinances and worship of God have a
claim on the household even prior to that of the
inter-domestic virtues. These things tend to
nourish the life whose fruit these virtues are.
The root is before the fruit.

It should become understood that, so far as
he can make it so, the Christian's home is held
as belonging to God; is a home where God is
worshipped, where His Word is held in honor

and put to daily use; in which also His ordinances are kept, and must be kept, by all who enter. A Bible should be in sight in almost every room. The cream of Christian literature should have the preference in purchases for the reading-table and the shelves. Christian hymns should at times be sung, Christian precepts should be cited and enforced, and appeal should be made to Christian motives. So far as the Christian is able, he should cause the whole atmosphere to be pervaded and hallowed by a Christian spirit, and all household law and habit to be based upon the divine law.

Especially does this responsibility rest upon Christian heads of families. The head of the household has authority; is responsible to God not only for self and for the wielding of influence, but also for the responsibility of rule. Such a one, whether husband or wife, is under bonds to see that God is openly and constantly recognized as Lord of the home: by the family service of prayer and praise; by invoking His guidance and protection; by seeking wisdom from His word; and by enforcing a respectful observance of His commands on all beneath the roof.

"Thou shalt teach these things to thy children."

"Remember the Sabbath-day to keep it holy. . . . on it thou shalt not do any work; thou, nor thy son, nor thy daughter, thy man-servant, nor thy maid-servant, nor thy cattle, *nor thy stranger that is within thy gates.*"

This responsibility is not to be shirked because it is difficult to bear: the duty is imperative. He who plays the coward in the presence of the responsibility, is unworthy of the honor, the privilege, which God bestowed in putting him in the place.

Let it be known that the home is held in a firm grasp, as a sacred trust from God; as one of His own ordinances, hallowed by His appointment and blessing, and made as sacred as the church. Let the sweet atmosphere of godliness surround all who enter, even for an hour; and go out with all who go, even for a hurried and formal call. Let the home be "sanctified," set apart, holy unto the Lord; with all its inmates, its influences, its opportunities, its responsibilities. Plan for the home. Pray for it. Work for it. Utilize it for Christ. Let it be the Master's dwelling-place.

III.

IN THE CHURCH.

" . . . that thou mayest know how thou oughtest to behave thyself in the house of God, which is the church of the living God, the pillar and stay of the truth."—1 Tim. iii. 15.

THE Christian should have a place in some Church of Christ. Translated, this is almost a truism. The original word for "church" means, simply, the assembly of those who have been "called out." Christ has "called out" His people from the world, "a peculiar people," unto Himself. The Christian is one of them. As a matter of course, his place is among them.

Baptism follows belief. Confession *of* Christ follows faith *in* Him. The inner substance seeks expression in the visible form. The believer should seek the society of believers. Those who are one in Christ should, as far as possible, manifest their unity together *with* Him: if Christ bind all together, they should be together in external association.

The promise and gift of the Holy Ghost to Christians, *as a power for aggression*, are to the church, not to the isolated believer : —

" Where two or three are gathered together in my name, there am I in the midst of them."

" And when the day of Pentecost was fully come, they were all with one accord in one place. And suddenly there came a sound from heaven, . . . and they were all filled with the Holy Ghost."

The early converts were received to the church: " And the Lord added unto the church daily such as should be saved." * The apostolic counsels to young Christians were addressed to the churches: " Paul . . . unto the church of God which is at Corinth;" " Paul . . . unto the churches of Galatia." In fine, there is nothing to indicate that the Scriptures contemplate the possibility of such a thing as a Christian remaining out of the visible fold for any appreciable length of time.

The Christian needs the fruits of church-membership. He is at first but a " babe " in

* Literally : " Added unto the church daily the saved."

Christ, — whatever he may *deem* himself. He requires protection and care. He needs the public song and prayer, the Baptism, and the Supper. He needs the stimulus and suggestion, the instruction and reproof, of the preached word. He needs the warmth of fellowship, the pastoral supervision and counsel, the repeated calls to labor, and the agency for benevolence, which the church was designed to supply. No Christian can afford to do without all this.

Some shrink: because, as they say, they are not worthy. — A wicked, swearing teamster, who had been the terror of his neighborhood, was converted. He was about to seek admission to the Lord's table. He was asked if he thought he was worthy. His answer was: —

"As worthy as any man; for I am a poor, worthless sinner, saved by the grace of God through the precious blood of Christ. I trust in Him alone."

No one has any other "worth" than Christ's; and all this is the portion of every believer. To speak of one's lack of worth, is either to doubt

Christ, or to forget that He is his who claims Him.

Many are staggered by a misconception as to the meaning of a single verse in Paul's recorded rebuke of the Corinthians.* These Christians had degraded the Supper into a Bacchanalian orgy. The apostle in the midst of the rebuke said, as translated: "He that eateth and drinketh unworthily, eateth and drinketh damnation to himself."

"Unworthily" many read "unworthy;" and the difference is vast! "Damnation" they read as it stands, without referring to the margin, where "judgment" (chastisement) is substituted; or to the context, where this is plainly shown: "For this cause many are weak and sickly among you, and many sleep." This was the chastisement upon the church for its folly: "But when we are judged, we are *chastened* of the Lord, that we should *not be condemned* with the world."

---

* 1 Cor. xi. 17–34. The whole passage must be taken together. Thus taken, and studied, it solves its own problems.

The church at Corinth turned the Supper into a midnight feast of gluttony and drunkenness. For *this* sin, the church was chastised by the loss of members in untimely death, and by an unusual and alarming sickness and infirmity among the living. This was because the Supper was observed unworthi-*ly*, — in a *manner* so unworthy. What, now, has all this to do with an isolated Christian ; one, too, who has no fear concerning his *method* of observance ? Simply nothing !

The ordinances of God's house are not so sacred that laying even a profane hand upon them puts one beyond reach of pardon. These ordinances may not, indeed, be treated with contumely, unrebuked. And what treatment, on the part of a trembling soul, could be more unworthy than studious neglect ! To refuse to partake is most dangerous. To disobey the divine command incurs risk: obedience brings blessing.

The weaker the Christian is, the more he needs the church. Why do men forget that Christ came to save *the lost !* The wayward and feeble have the strongest claim upon these sacred provisions, — at least until they plunge into wanton disobedience or open disgrace. Christ's way with such is thus declared: " The bruised reed will He not break, and the smoking flax will He not quench, till He bring forth judgment unto victory." *

This membership is a privilege. No man confers a favor on a church by uniting with it. The youngest, the feeblest, the most obscure church, in the Master's name confers a favor on the noblest, the wealthiest, the most cultured, the most influential man, when he is welcomed to its fellowship. This is a privilege, however, which may not justly be withheld from any of Christ's own — who strive to live to Him — when they come knocking at the door.

The church needs the Christian. He should come that he may *do* good, as well as get good. There is room in this field of good-doing, for

* In the whole realm of Christian literature there is perhaps nothing more admirable, in its way, than the sermon of President Davies on " The Compassion of Christ to weak Believers," founded on this text. Vol I., Ser. viii.

even "little folk." Jesus said "the Lord hath need of him," even of an ass. The most obscure person is needed in the place to which the Master calls him; and, perhaps in ways he cannot discern, he will be of use there. The use may be small, but is real; and it is essential. The house requires its doorstep, humble as is its office; and the little lath, small as it is and unseen of men. The church is not complete while there is lacking the presence of the humblest person whom God calls to a place in its midst.

The church-membership should be located, and kept or changed, on the basis of God's call. One's place is where God wants him; not necessarily where he wants to go. God may want His child in some church which has heavy financial burdens to bear, a hard fight to make in acquiring a foothold, a large amount of evangelistic work to do, an untrained membership requiring culture, a poverty-stricken people awaiting assistance, or a disheartened minister needing stimulus and aid. It may be that where such wants are to be found, there the Christian will find his own best development as well as his greatest usefulness. How few try the experiment! The natural choice is apt to be upon other principles ; but the "natural" choice is the choice of men, a guess, a hazard in the dark. The Christian should walk in the Light, going where God calls.

Wherever he may be, *the Christian should help bear the burdens of the church.* He need not be forward, but he should be ready. Refusal or neglect to share these burdens, is dishonesty.

There is even more need, oftentimes, of the presence, the votes, the counsels, *the thinking-force*, the labors, the gifts, — of the humble, the poor, and the inexpert, than of the similar services of the wise, the adepts, the men of prominence. Yet the more one might accomplish by the effort, the greater is the robbery of his brethren if he withhold it. There are attorneys as guilty of theft in this way as, in another line merely, are some of the rogues whom they prosecute. There are merchants as guilty thus, as their peculating clerks are otherwise. Spartan morality is not yet extinct, even in our churches : " The crime is not in doing wrong, but in being caught."

The women are needed in the assemblages and work of the church, as well as the men. The business meetings of the congregation have claims on all. The finances appeal to the poorest. The prayer-meetings lay requirements on those whose gifts are least cultivated. " The little things are the great things : " no one may excuse himself by saying, " I am not much."

The hosts of Christians who neglect the social gathering commit a grave wrong. And the still greater hosts who relegate the Sabbath-school to more willing hands, are agents in permitting and committing an injury which may yet send its thrill of pain through all the churches of the land, and perhaps even result in their undermining and prostration ! The careless wielding of the vast responsibilities imposed upon Christians in our time by this peculiar work, and the complete neglect of which some

11   P

of our most stable people are guilty, have already given rise to grave problems, and to some alarming indications. The most precious interests of truth are as much involved in the character of our Sabbath-school teaching, as in the orthodoxy of our schools of theology; and the *healthy* growth of the church has, through the prevalent neglect of domestic training, come to be involved as much in evangelistic work for and in the Sabbath-school, as in all that the average pulpit can accomplish. Let the Christian be sure of his warrant for absence from this scene of evangelism and Christian culture.

The Christian's aim in the church, and for the church, should be Christ-like. In seeking his own profit, his aim should be " doctrine, reproof, instruction, correction in righteousness, that the man of God may be perfect, thoroughly furnished unto all good works; " together with needed comfort and support. He should expect, relish, and profit by "reproof," and even " rebuke; " nor permit himself to grow sore and become alienated when they are administered.

The Master, knowing the needs of His people, has provided explicit commands for His ministers : —

"These things teach, and exhort, and rebuke with all authority. Let no man despise thee."

"Put them in mind . . . "

"Preach the word, . . . reprove, rebuke, exhort, with all long-suffering and doctrine."

The church should never be used as a mere comfortable place of resort, as an agency of æsthetic culture or gratification, as an intellectual luxury, or as a carnal convenience. The church is God's ordinance, sacred to high uses. It should be sought to make it the agency of the greatest possible spiritual blessings. It should be kept in such condition as to reach all whom God gives it the opportunity of reaching, whether they be rich or poor, learned or illiterate. Tastes should be restrained, personal enjoyment deferred, and personal preference held in check, — in all matters of form and conduct, — whenever such self-sacrifice would justly give the church a wider sweep of influence.

It was not designed that any local church should be used as the property of its members, — open to additions from congenial quarters, but practically closed to others. Every church has a *mission;* and God only can give its direction or set its limits. The church is to be in readiness to do all that lies at hand to be done, if any self-sacrifice will accomplish it.

Further: each member has his share of responsibility for the presentation of truth from the pulpit, and the culture and maintenance of integrity in the pews. These things should be to him objects of desire, prayer, and determination. The faithful preaching of the truth, — even in the midst of opposition, — and the maintenance of discipline among the members, should not be resented. They should be encouraged. Welcome an antagonism which speaks of fidelity amid human folly! Let us exult in that God is pleased to make His sword so effective in our hands as to create antagonism. The hands of ministers and officers should be held up in the face of such opposition. No Christian should

flinch in time of trial, of dissension, of popular
tumult. Popularity is the poorest possible test
of success.

Aggressive movements, taking various directions, operating by labors and by gifts, should
ever be encouraged. It is not the part of a
disciple of Jesus to resent appeals, though they
be frequent and urgent, for contributions to
benevolence. No follower of Him who said,
" Go ye into all the world," should ignore or
depreciate the claims of Foreign Missions. Nor
can the disciple of Him who always went about
doing good, rightly evade a call to any task
which God may set before him, or strive to
withhold the church when its corporate effort
is required. A mission-school, for instance,
may be a heavy burden for some churches to
carry ; yet that consideration is not final against
founding and maintaining it.

The member should eagerly desire the church
to be a faithful representative of Him whose
activity was ceaseless, and most fatiguing ; who
preached the law in its sternest forms ; who

gave the most minute and personal delineations of sin, and visited it with the most scathing rebukes; who upheld the truth of God, preaching doctrines most humbling to the human heart, and most fruitful in exciting anger and enmity; who was found in company with all classes of men, accommodating himself to the needs of each; who shrunk from no sacrifice, and asked no selfish ease, when engaged in his Father's business.

The spirit of the Christian, in all his behavior in the church, should be that of his Master. His speech, his conduct, his very demeanor, should at every point betray Christ-likeness.

Fault-findings with the brethren, envy, piques, pride, self-seeking, the assertion of one's rights, a readiness to take offence, even secret dissatisfaction upon being or seeming ignored, should find no place. Let every evil tendency be put down with a strong hand: whoever fails in this must suffer from the failure.

Love of the brethren should be manifest. Patience, pity, sympathy, counsel, assistance, should be freely rendered. Cordial greetings should be frequent: they should not be with-held even when the laws of Society require it. Christ's claims are prior.

The rule implied in the words, " Then they that feared the Lord spake often one to an-other," is susceptible of very wide application. There are comparatively few churches in which every member should not feel obliged to know every other member, and to make early ac-quaintance with every one who enters after his own reception. The acquaintance and the greeting should reach out beyond, — to mere attendants, and to others who are in the poten-tial constituency of the church. And the fail-ure to procure frequent assemblages for social purposes, can scarcely pass unrebuked.

It is very questionable whether the stiffness begotten by the habits of modern society, should be permitted to repress or forbid the grasp of the hand in salutation. It certainly is now omitted to an unjust and injurious extent. Is there not here a needed token of brother-hood? " We are many members of one body."

"And He gave some . . . pastors and teachers, for the perfecting of the saints, . . . for the edifying of the body of Christ. Till we all come . . . unto a perfect man ; . . . that we henceforth be no more children, . . . but speaking the truth in love, may grow up into Him in all things, which is the Head, even Christ; from whom the whole body, fitly joined together and compacted by that which every joint supplieth, according to the effectual working in the measure of every part, maketh increase of the body, unto the edifying of itself in love. . . . Let all bitterness, and wrath, and anger, and clamor, and evil-speaking be put away from you, with all malice ; and be ye kind one to another, tender-hearted, forgiving one another, even as God for Christ's sake hath forgiven you."

IV.

AMONG MEN.

" That ye may be blameless and harmless, the sons of God without rebuke, in the midst of a crooked and perverse nation, among whom ye shine as lights in the world." — Phil. ii. 15.

WITHDRAWAL from a busy life, in order to enter the service of God, is a mistake. The Master said, " I pray not that thou shouldst take them out of the world." Both the spirit and the explicit command of the gospel, require the presence of Christians among men; and that in their true character, as sons of God.

" Ye are the light of the world; let your light so shine among men."

" . . . in the midst of a crooked and perverse nation, among whom ye shine as lights in the world."

The meaning of these and kindred injunctions is unmistakable. The Christian is to transmit the light, the thought, the spirit of Christ

11*

among men under all circumstances. He should never act for self, as self. He is ever the representative of Christ, even when engaged in the most commonplace affairs. His rights, as his own; his convenience, comfort, worldly prosperity, — may never give the law to his aim or his conduct. All he does should be done in his Master's name, with His direction, and in the power of His Spirit.

A young Christian, on receiving such counsel as this, once said : —

" That is all very well, and very right no doubt; but a man doing business on such principles could never succeed in the world ! "

That depends, in part, on what is meant by success. Success is not to be measured by acres, weighed with gold, or tested by human huzzas. A man may die poor and unknown, after passing life in narrow circumstances and unobserved places, and yet have achieved the grandest success: he may have honored his Master in his appointed place, from first to last. The poor cobbler through whose unpolished words Guizot's infidelity was overthrown, was a successful man; yet he probably died poor, and his name is not held in remembrance. Success is pleasing Christ!

But it is not true that a close walk with God prevents the acquisition of wealth, influence, or fame. On the contrary, the surest way to these ends, and to the sustained possession of these gifts, is the way of Light. What the Christian gains, he is apt to keep; and he is fitted to enjoy it as no other can do.

Men have curiously blundered into the notion that Christianity tends to make a man a simpleton. It is rashly inferred that a severely conscientious Christian is liable to be wheedled at every turn because he is commanded to think no evil, to indulge no suspicions of men's motives, to refrain from judging men; that he is liable to be imposed on because he dare not assert himself, insist upon his "rights," resent injuries, hate his enemies, or even push his own interests; that he is secure of poverty because he is under obligation to refrain from tricks of trade, from violating the Sabbath for the sake of his business, from receiving gain from schemes involving wickedness, and because he is under peculiar obligations of benevolence, and of charity to needy debtors.

" I must suspect every man I deal with," said Mr. N——, " or I should be cheated constantly, and must end in bankruptcy."

Not at all. It is only because business is conducted on principles and by methods condemned by the Scriptures, that there is any great danger of such disaster. The rules and methods of business — and the restraint upon the personal and domestic expenditures which draw upon and exhaust the business — should be such as to keep men safe. If men were always to practise the frugality which the Scriptures command, if they would resolutely *force* all expenditure, personal or domestic, within such limits as the business will legitimately allow, the vast majority of the anxieties of which men complain would be avoided, and many of the failures averted. " We must live ! "

is usually a dishonest plea for unnecessary indulgence. The most stringent economy is better than dishonesty; bread and water, than bankruptcy.

"Have no confidence in the flesh" is an injunction tending not to personal suspicion (save of self), but to a rational recognition of the fallen state of *all* men. Hence it points to the need of such general methods of dealing, as will provide for the manifest conditions of safe commerce.

The Book which commands men, "Be ye wise as serpents;" which says, "The simple believeth every word, but the prudent man looketh well to his going," and "confidence in an unfaithful man in time of trouble, is like a broken tooth and a foot out of joint;" the Book which warns against complications, against debts, against prodigality, against sloth; which says, "As a bird that wandereth from her nest, so is a man that wandereth from his place," saying this by way of exhibiting the folly of neglect; and which adds, "Be thou diligent to know the state of thy flocks, and look well to thy herds ; " the Book which discountenances suretyships, partnerships with vicious men, connection with or dependence upon an iniquitous vocation, and which in many other directions utters repeated and pungent counsels concerning the very things in which lie the great dangers of commercial life, — this is not a book which can be justly charged with making men simpletons in the business-world.

The difficulty lies in not wholly obeying the Scriptures. Men try to walk at the same time on both sides of the chasm which separates the paths of darkness and Light. They want to be " *a little* worldly." They try to live as Christians, yet they ignore the prudential maxims, and the rich, practical wisdom, which Christianity supplies, while they employ instead, the wisdom of this world. Their motto is " Religion is religion, and business is business ! " " Ye *cannot* serve God and Mammon," says the Word. If men will not entirely break connection with the world, they may expect to be dragged down. They might win a certain "success" as worldlings: they may nobly succeed as Christians. But the two forms and methods of success will not coalesce; each mars the other.

Ko-San-Lone, a Chinese convert, when in America on a visit, was impressed with the striking similarity between the style of living maintained by Christians, and that of men of the world. Adverting to this he said : —

" When the disciples in my country come out from the world, *they come clear out!* "

The divergence of external habit may not need to be at every point so manifest here, as there; since, with us, the world patterns much after Christian forms; and apes our progress; yet here, as in China, if Christians will succeed, they must " come clear out."

So long as men are content to be implicated in the iniquitous liquor-traffic, however remotely; so long as they seek wealth by drawing dividends from Sabbath-breaking associations; so long as their prosperity is permitted to depend, essentially and knowingly, upon the conduct or fortunes of men engaged in any nefarious occupation, or of men known to be destitute of principle; so long as merchants will employ dishonest clerks for the purpose of "shoving" their wares, and clerks serve employers whose business is fundamentally unrighteous; so long as men will "make haste to be rich," taking undue risks, trading far beyond their capital and making many complications, rather than choose the slower path of safety, — they need not be surprised to find themselves coming far short of sustained and satisfactory success, and in most cases they may look for humiliating failure; while also their "light" will yield but a feeble and flickering illumination.

A mechanic once said to a Christian friend : —

"A man cannot work at this trade without telling lies. Only this morning I promised a man that I should do his work this week. I do not see how I can get it done. But if I had not promised, I should have lost the job. What is a man to do ? "

The conversation was reported to one who had formerly followed the same occupation. He said : —

"He is right! and that is why I quit the business."

And he who had left his trade and saved his integrity, was in less straitened circumstances than he who had kept his business at the sacrifice of principle.

If, in any community, any line of business become so corrupted that honesty is quite crowded out, honest men have no choice : they must go out also. But it may be doubted whether, in most cases at least, honesty would not do better by refusing to be crowded out, by biding its time and reaping its fruits, — tardy perhaps, but rich.

The master of a shop once said : —

"There is no use trying to be a Christian in this business, in this town, while —— keeps a shop. He will cut down prices, and then put in poor stuff! I would sell out if I could; meanwhile, I must make a living."

Q

He soon sold out ; but it is by no means certain that he did not refuse a call of Providence to do a needed work, — to reform a corrupted trade throughout an entire community, by standing firm himself. Any one called to such a task will find himself enabled, perhaps in some surprising way, to tide over the evil hour until the time come for the unmasking and dethronement of vice, and for the discovery and rewarding of honesty. The eagerness to " get on," however, becomes absorbing. Christians too often forget the moral ends to be served by their vocation, in the material ends.

Mr. O——, a contractor, was a severely conscientious man, and a member of the church. Entering into competition for employment, he soon found inferior work so much in vogue that he must either make his margins for profit small, or be content to see his bids rejected. His competition was seldom successful, and his profits were always meagre. Yet he did not desert his chosen vocation. He could do nothing but plod on, submit to life in straitened circumstances, make sure of his petty savings, and present thorough work. In thirty years he had achieved a position in the esteem of those who knew him, such as few reach. His church-membership was honorable and useful ; his very character lent stability to the body. Except in grace, his attainments were limited. His voice was seldom heard in religious address. His public prayers were uttered with a stammering tongue. He was not given to aggressive Christian work. Yet his influence on behalf of the Cross grew steadily stronger among all who knew him. What reformation of false methods of business he may have effected in the line of his vocation, cannot be told ; his own habits suffered no change. He did not grow rich ; but he became able to live in the enjoyment of solid comfort, to provide unusually well for the pleasure and the culture of his household, and to help carry many a heavy burden of the church; and he was blessed with one of the most delightful families, — every member of it a Christian, — and one of the happiest and most attractive homes, to be found anywhere.

With slight variations in unessential particulars, this minute characterization will apply to each of five men in the limited acquaintance of a single observer. The coincidence is significant: Christianity tends to produce just such men; and when she has produced them, she is apt to use and honor them in very similar ways. There are doubtless thousands of these sturdy Christians scattered over the land, " unostentatious, quiet men, humble mechanics," whose presence imparts new sturdiness to almost as many churches, and whose success in life is of the most satisfying nature.

It is said, apparently on good authority, that of every one hundred men who engage in merchandising, ninety-seven sooner or later fail. Yet the following facts are vouched for on authority equally good: In a few small and contiguous communities in a certain narrow section of country, there are nine merchants who have prosecuted their calling without interruption, and with steady success, for many years. The most of them have grown gray.

Some of them have practically withdrawn from active life. Each began life poor, and has become rich. While their past and present methods obtain, it is impossible that any one of them should fail. Several of these men are widely honored office-bearers in the church. Every one of them has had the benefit of a thorough Christian training, especially in respect of those matters of honest and honorable dealing and frugal living which the Scriptures so frequently and so forcibly command. Every one of them is noted for his unflinching and unbroken adherence to principle, his economy of expenditure, and his avoidance of the excitement, complications, over-trading and hasting to be rich, which are characteristic of the times. Not one of them is penurious; nearly all are deemed liberal; the most of them are termed "open-handed;" and two or three seem almost lavish in their gifts to the churches and the standard agencies of benevolence.

These men also are but instances of what Christianity is everywhere producing; and their lives are but a few of the hosts of real and apt illustrations of the rich material success which is perfectly consonant with a minute observance of God's law, which is apt to be produced by that observance, and which is always best maintained and most fully enjoyed by those who have thus legitimately achieved it.

It is a slander upon our holy religion to charge it with making men idiots and blunderers, as some by implication do. There is no keener shrewdness than that which godliness fosters, tends to produce, and very often does produce, — ever tempering it with kindliness, and denying it the sting of an animating selfishness.

There is no other such firmness in the emergencies of life, and against the enticements of illusory schemes, as that which comes by the transfusion of the will of God into the human brain, and which first operates by enabling its possessor to say, resolutely, No! to every temptation to sin, and to every suggestion of an unworthy principle of action. There is no other

such " grit," as that which deep-seated righteousness tends to develop; no other such
enterprise, such energy, as are attained by him
who hears from his Lord the word, " Not
slothful in business, . . . serving the Lord,"
and, " Seest thou a man diligent in his business?
he shall stand before kings; he shall not stand
before mean men." There is no other such prudence, as that of him who knows he is a stew-
ard of Jesus Christ, who is determined to please
Him at any cost, and who hears Him say, " A
prudent man foreseeth the evil, and hideth
himself." There is no steadiness, whether of
standing or of aim, equal to his whose feet rest
consciously upon the Rock of Ages, and whose
eye is fixed upon the hope of the righteous " at
His appearing." There is no vigor like his
whose life is ever renewed by a flow from the
strength of the Lord of life; no keenness of
vision like his who walks in the Light; no
other such unyielding pertinacity of purpose,
as his whose devotion is daily baptized and
renewed by the Holy Ghost; no other such

resolute daring — when the emergency requires it — as his who always dares do what God requires; no wisdom in dealing with men, like that which comes from Him who knows the nature of men. There is no breadth of view — a thing in some sort so essential to success in human vocations — equal to that acquired by walking with Him who views all things; no other such fulness and readiness of resource, in the times of trial which try the souls of business men, as that of him who is able to draw in a moment upon the resources of the Infinite One; no other such uncompromising and successful maintenance of one's rights, as that of him who cares nothing for his rights as such, but holds them sacred for his Master, and who pushes or maintains them only when duty requires, "for His sake;" as when Paul, in prison at Philippi, — for the sake of Christ's cause, — stood resolutely upon the dignity of his Roman citizenship, until the rulers became alarmed and *besought* him to depart.

And there is no other such rich enjoyment of

"success," as that of him who has sought it solely that he might lay it at the Master's feet, laboring for and confidently expecting His approval.

In a word: abiding in Christ, and the abiding of His words in the soul, tend, not to make men simpletons, but to make men wise; not to make them failures, but to make them eminently successful; and, above all, not to leave them dissatisfied and restless during the struggle, and even after it is over, but to produce in them peace and contentment meanwhile, and afterward to crown them with the richest sense of triumph and satisfaction in view of what *Grace* has enabled them to achieve. The Christian life is the highest style of life, in every good sense of the term.

As statesmen, Joseph and Daniel were marvels of success; their success came through the wisdom they obtained direct from God, through their unflinching adherence to principle, and through their unyielding determination to serve "the God of heaven," openly, even — in Dan-

12

iel's case — in the face of savage and relentless opposition.

Rural life has seen no grander success than that of Abraham, and no more ignominious and astounding failure than that of Lot. Yet, at the turning-point of life, it was Lot who grasped at — and gained — manifest and unsurpassed worldly advantage, while Abraham as willingly relinquished it. But the worldly advantage was at the expense of evil companionships, and the consequent deterioration of character and looseness of life.

The greatest trials through which Rebekah and Jacob were called to pass, were the direct result of their use of worldly methods to secure a rightful privilege and prerogative.

The unparalleled successes of Moses, were all gained by a rigid following of minute and immediate directions from God. And yet men say that such a life makes a man a puppet! If Moses was a puppet, the estate is dignified beyond reproach, by the greatness he achieved, the merit he displayed, and the results he won.

Probably, all things considered, the most successful general — and certainly the man whose name and memory are held in highest esteem and warmest affection — in the armies of the South in our late civil war, was one, the secret of whose vigor, energy, daring, and resoluteness, in no small part lay in his daily walking with God; whose success could not have been so rich, but for the maintenance of a pure conscience on all occasions. General Thomas J. Jackson was a man of might, because he knew and utilized " the secret of the Lord," and walked accordingly. Even his nickname, *Stonewall*, fitly characterizes the rocky firmness which Grace is wont to impart to the human will.

The late Commodore Foote, U.S.N., was a devoted Christian, steady and sturdy in his maintenance of the Christian character, in his devotion to Christian ends throughout his official life, — in a sphere from which Christian ends are commonly supposed to be excluded, — and in his use of life for his Master's service alone. It is remarkable that his promotion was, in several instances, distinctly traceable to acts which Conscience bade him perform, against the dictates of worldly wisdom, and in the face of the gravest opposition.

Christ makes men MEN, — not blunderers, simpletons, machines, or bigots, — such men as the world needs and will honor, — however tardily; men who are needed "among men," in every honorable vocation; men who will succeed in life, and whose success will bring them a sweet satisfaction, and the approval of Him who has lovingly commanded his disciples : —

" That ye may be blameless, and harmless, the sons of God without rebuke, in the midst of a crooked and perverse nation, *among whom* ye shine as LIGHTS in the world."

PART FIFTH.

——◆——

WORKING IN THE LIGHT.

(Christian Labor.)

————

"Son, go work to-day in my vineyard." — Matt. xxi. 28.

I. Responsibility.

II. Hinderances.

III. Motives.

IV. What to do.

———

" The harvest truly is plenteous, but the LABORERS are few ;
pray ye, therefore, the Lord of the harvest, that He would send
forth laborers into His harvest." — MATT. ix. 37, 38.

I.

RESPONSIBILITY.

"And he called his ten servants, and delivered them ten pounds, and said unto them, Occupy till I come." — LUKE xix. 13.

WHEN Saul of Tarsus became a follower of Jesus, while he yet lay upon the ground, his first words were: "Lord, what wilt thou have me to do?"

This was not the anxious inquiry of one in search of safety, and addressing men, as was that of the Philippian jailer, "Men and brethren, what must I do to be saved?" It was the eager question of one who knew his salvation, who recognized the voice of his Master and Lord, and whose first thought was of serving Him.

It is related that an English nobleman, travelling on the Mediterranean, was once passenger on a ship manned by rude men and sometimes employed in schemes of iniquity. He discovered a fellow-passenger who seemed disconsolate. It was ascertained that he was a slave, destined to the most barbarous service in Morocco. The Englishman found the captor, brought him face to face with the slave, demanded that a ransom be named, and paid it, — £200. The disheartened captive could scarcely realize his good fortune. After a moment, out of his confusion there dawned upon him a sense of his freedom and of the kindness that had been shown him; whereupon he prostrated himself at the feet of the nobleman, and said: "I thank you! Every drop of blood in my body thanks you! I will be your servant for ever!"

A Christian who had long walked in darkness, having at length been led to a discovery of the nature and security of his standing before God, in Christ Jesus, said : —

"I cannot but love Him. Who would not love the matchless Jesus if he only knew Him? How different I find loving Him, from merely reverencing and respecting Him! How different to love Himself, from loving, in a kind of way, his religion!"

> " Oh, for such love, let rocks and hills
>   Their lasting silence break ;
> And all harmonious human tongues
>   The Saviour's praises speak ! "

> " A soul redeemed demands a life of praise ;
>   *Hence* the complexion of its future days."

This is the argument of the apostle when he says : —

" I beseech you therefore, brethren, *by the mercies of God*, that ye present your bodies a living sacrifice, holy, acceptable unto God, which is your reasonable service."

It is reasonable both to ask, and to expect, such full consecration and such eager devotion ; because the soul is bought with blood, redeemed from terrific and eternal woe, and unspeakably blessed and exalted in the Redeemer.

This devotion sometimes becomes a marvel. Indeed, the words " a living sacrifice," imply that it should always pass the bounds of *calculating* service. It is not unreasonable to expect the Christian to become " a man of one purpose, the glory of God ; a fool, and content to be a fool, for Christ ; a madman, and content to be reckoned a madman, for Christ." *

* Edward Irving.

12*   R

Paul was twice accused of madness. And no wonder; for such was his absorbing zeal, that he counted it joy to suffer for Christ's sake : —

"Therefore I take pleasure in infirmities, in reproaches, in necessities, in persecutions, in distresses for Christ's sake."

"In stripes above measure, in prisons more frequent, in deaths oft. Of the Jews five times received I forty stripes save one. Thrice was I beaten with rods, once was I stoned, thrice I suffered shipwreck, a night and a day have I been in the deep : in journeyings often, in perils of waters, in perils of robbers, in perils by mine own countrymen, in perils by the heathen, in perils in the city, in perils in the wilderness, in perils in the sea, in perils among false brethren ; in weariness and painfulness ; in watchings often ; in hunger and thirst, in fastings often, in cold and nakedness. . . . If I must needs glory, I will glory in the things which concern mine infirmities."

When charged with folly in all this, the apostle's sublime and simple answer was : "The love of Christ *constraineth* us."

Would that we had thousands of such *madmen*, fired with a consuming zeal, fed on the "matchless love," and careless of consequences in the Master's service. The church needs them; the souls of the dying need them; and the cause of Christ languishes because we have so few of them. Let the record and the appeals of Paul, enter the chambers of our Christian common sense. Strip from them the false glamour of distance; let the records have the force of placing the apostle by the side of the ordinary Christian of to-day; let him be regarded as but one of us, as he was, — a sinner saved by grace. What was reasonable for Paul, is reasonable for Christians now. What zeal was demanded of him, is demanded of us; what repression or denial of it would have been treachery in him, is treachery still.

It is not merely that gratitude calls to this service. The Christian is His representative, and the partaker of His nature who said: "The zeal of thine house *hath eaten me up;*" "My meat is to do the will of Him that sent me, and to finish His work." The position and privilege of one who holds this place, are such that he has no choice, in honor. He should be all this — or nothing!

The humblest believer is a light-bearer; is a representative of Him who proclaimed Himself the Light of the world. He is a servant, left upon the estate in the absence of its Lord, charged with its management and enlargement until He return. He is one of those to whom were given the words : —

"Ye are my witnesses."

"What I tell you in darkness, that speak ye in light; and what ye hear in the ear, that preach ye upon the house-tops."

"Go ye into all the world, and preach the gospel to every creature."

The Christian is set for the defence of the Cross ; for the maintenance of the truth ; for the proclamation of the help and healing which the Cross affords. He is a son of God, in immediate and loving fellowship with his Elder Brother, and with his Heavenly Father : as such, he has Christ's place to fill, and Christ's work to do!

This responsibility cannot be evaded. One may say : " I had rather be a doorkeeper; I do not aspire to the position of a son of God, a representative of Christ. I do not claim such joy, so rich a salvation. I have not asked so much as this from Christ."

No matter. There is no choice. There is no other position provided for the Christian. There is no less rich, or less complete salvation offered. It is not humility, but indolence, that seeks the escape; and there is no escape. One stands in this precise position, — side by side with Paul, — or he does not stand in Christ. The dilemma is thrust upon the soul, — the " high calling," or no Christ ! There is no *tiers état*, no third estate. There is ruin, utter and terrific ; and there is salvation, glorious and complete, fully bestowed the instant Christ is accepted. There is " the service of sin," and there is " the service of righteousness." The man must make his choice, *here ;* and abide by it !

" . . . because we thus judge, that if One died for all, then were all *dead;* and that He died for all, that they which *live*, should not henceforth live unto themselves, but unto Him which died for them, and rose again."

As for those who do not so live, it can only be said that they lead an inconsistent life: " they are rich, but they live like beggars."

So long as our Lord delay his return, all Christians have His work to do: each one has some part in it. It was not meant that all the time and thought of any should be taken up with the ordinary cares and pursuits of life. It was not designed that a chosen few should have the privilege of exhibiting the power of love to spur to action, and to sustain in endurance; the privilege of zeal for God's house, of spreading the honor of the Cross, of defending the truth and winning souls.

After the walk, comes work: after living for Christ, comes laboring for Him. Because a warfare is upon us. Good soldiers of Jesus Christ are needed at many a beleaguered point. The truth needs myriad tongues to utter it. The Cross needs myriad hands, to raise it aloft and to hold it up. " The sword of the Spirit, which is the word of God," waits to be wielded by myriad arms. And every Christian is urged, and enjoined, to take this sword, — having first ".put on the armor of Light."

II.

HINDERANCES.

"There is a lion in the way; a lion is in the streets."—Prov. xxvi. 13.

" I WOULD, but . . . "

The soul that is called to work for Christ, is almost certain to stumble upon some hinderance. "There is a lion in the way; a lion is in the streets," is a frequent cry. But it is the cry of one who has not gone boldly up to the lion. The lion is there, but he is chained and toothless, — able to frighten by his roar when one is at a distance, but unable to hurt when one draws near. The "mountains of difficulty" are but molehills, relatively: God's provisions of help rise towering above them. The clouds which obscure the road, and frighten the inexpert traveller, are but fog and vapor: they will break and vanish beneath the beams of the Sun of Righteousness. *Light* makes all things plain.

In the very nature of the case, the hinderances, at the worst, cannot be great enough, grievous enough, or sufficiently numerous, to prevent continuous and even joyful service. God makes no vain calls upon His children, lays on them no impossible requirements: "I can do *all* things, through Christ, which strengtheneth me."

God may hedge up the way in certain directions, but He leaves it open elsewhere. The problem is to find where. The certainty is that there is somewhere a gap in the hedge. It is true that "they also serve who only stand and wait;" but in such cases the waiting is imposed, not voluntary; and the very repression of desire which it produces, causes the emission of a grateful perfume, as from a trodden flower, of which the Master just then has need, and which He will put to noble use. Is the soul that shrinks back, waiting to be bruised and *crushed?*

Hinderances are a help! They sometimes hedge up a way which, for the soul in question, would lead to unseen dangers, and perhaps grave disaster. The Christian needs to seek another avenue of endeavor, not to turn his back on all.

Sometimes, however, it is designed that they be overcome. In such cases, the effort to overcome serves to develop a vigor of virtue which will stand its possessor in good stead on other fields and other days.

No one should say, " I cannot," when God calls. " As thy days, so shall thy strength be." " My grace is sufficient for thee; for my strength is made perfect in weakness." These are God's promises. Can God lie ? In one's self, one is — nothing ; in Christ, — every thing that God requires. One's own strength is weakness; and therein is God's strength " made perfect." " Most gladly, therefore, will I rather *glory* in my infirmities, that the power of Christ may rest upon me."

There are *entanglements*. Some of these must be broken, at whatever cost. One should count the cost before choosing Christ as King: there is no room for calculation afterwards. God's gift was boundless. It calls for unhesitating, uncalculating devotion, in return. Any thing less is unworthy and irrational.

Some entanglements must be borne. It will not always do to cut the Gordian knot: honor and honesty may prevent. Where any interest beyond one's own is involved, to sacrifice it ruthlessly for the sake of "serving Christ," is apt to be sheer selfishness. Sometimes the longing for a special or a wider "field," proves to be a foolish, boyish, carnal passion, and it needs the imperative hinderance to chasten and restrain it. Some ardent young men and women have been hindered from becoming Foreign Missionaries, — without the least damage to the heathen! There is every now and then a tidal wave of influence bearing men on uncalled into some special channel of Christian work: Satan often produces *manias* in the church. Most young Christians are at some time or other tempted to a great wrong under the specious and false plea of "giving up all for Christ." These are counterfeits of Christian enthusiasm. True Christian madness is methodical and judicious; it waits for God's call; it does not spring from "gush," but from a long study, a broad wisdom, and a deep-seated conviction; so that one is driven to the self-sacrifice, — somewhat as was Paul when he said, " Wo is me if I preach *not* the gospel."

The most are wanted for the common walks of life, to adorn them and make them fragrant with " a sweet savor of Christ." They should find room for work close by the side of their daily toil. Only the few are called to extraordinary paths: it is well that imperative hinderances exist for others. Entanglements of home, of kindred, of debt, and the like, are apt to be binding, to be the entanglements of honor and honesty. And they are blessings. They are not meant to prevent all toil, but only mistaken effort. Look elsewhere.

Weakness sometimes hinders. It is well: " Weakness is strength! " Go forward. Draw upon the resources of the Infinite One.

When weakness is urged as an excuse for inaction, the plea is a covert falsehood, so subtle that he who makes it is himself deceived by it. Whoever feels his weakness as it is, despairs of self, leans wholly on his Lord, and is immediately strengthened up to his full need. He who feels strong enough to stand still, but not strong enough to go forward, does not know how weak he is! He cannot stand still : he needs God's strength to hold him ; and, having that, he has all, — he can advance!

Weakness is a legitimate plea only against that to which God does not call; and, if one determine that any specific request from men for service is not "of God," there rests on him the immediate responsibility of finding some other line of labor ; for God calls every Christian to do something. "Go work," is universal: "And to every man his work."

Evil habits hinder many. There is but one thing for such persons to do : these habits must be ground to atoms beneath the heel of sacred resolve, planted upon them by the resistless will of God, which is the believer's resort and strength. The task is possible. Even the drunkard may reform. No evil habit is invincible, in the presence of Grace.

The lack of habit restrains some, — from public prayer; from address; from giving the word of counsel or of comfort in private; from social duty in the Master's name. The habit should be cultivated. The means are at our disposal. Especially, "practice makes perfect." Small success may be expected at first, but pride must bow. The day of small things must be endured: it cannot be leaped. One must begin with little efforts, attended perhaps with humiliating blunders. There is no growth without beginning. "Despise not the day of small things," nor make that "day" perpetual. "Attain." "Press forward."

Human opposition sometimes arises. "All that will live godly in Christ Jesus shall suffer persecution." We share with Christ the world's antagonism. Even one's own friends, perhaps his pastor or his brethren in the church, may rise in opposition to his purest endeavors for the Master.

Nevertheless, " we ought to obey God rather than men." If, upon revision of the scheme in the larger light afforded by the opposition, the call of God still seem plain, let the difficulty but provoke a sterner resolve and a more persistent execution. The opposition will call the more attention to the work, and perhaps make the achievement more fruitful.

It may not be designed that achievement result. The endeavor may be irresistibly stopped at a certain point. Still, if called for up to that point, it will be used. God delights in using our fragments. He seldom permits men to round off their work to completeness. John Baptist was stopped : as then judged, his work was a fragment; but what a glorious fragment!

Sometimes the success of the opposition is designed, even against the endeavor which was also designed: God employs opposing forces. In such cases, the pent-up resolve is sure to find vent in some other channel, perhaps in some strange, unique, marvellously successful work.

John Bunyan was called to preach, was effectually stopped midway — by prison-bars. But
the constraining love still boiled in his veins;
preach he would, — if not with the tongue, by
the pen. Hence " Bunyan's Pilgrim's Progress," an achievement of success in the service
of Christ which, in its line, probably stands without a parallel since the days of the apostles.
" Surely the wrath of man shall praise thee."

It sometimes seems to the worker that God
Himself is against him. He seems to thrust
obstacles in the way — " almost wantonly,"
wails the weak soul. He thwarts plans which
had been prayerfully and carefully matured.
Sometimes when success seems near, when hope
is highest, when patient toil seems about to reap
fruition, and joy stands waiting just at the birth,
He hurls the choice design to earth in ruins.
The morbid fancy suggests that He appears to
take delight in thwarting the holiest human
ambitions.

Not so. The cherished scheme might have
wrought grievous disaster, to its operator or to

others. It might have restrained the arm from something more needful or more fitting. And in God's hands the unsightly ruins, the vision of which gives such exquisite pain, will be seen to take on a beauty all their own. There is no harshness here : God is not unfeeling, nor unwise. His eye falls lovingly on the *intended* service, and even on the shattered fragments of the cherished design. His Providence will make glorious use of what seems useless now, and wasted.

The temptations of the Adversary hinder. These are hinderances of quite another sort. They sometimes prove the destruction of the whole fabric of a useful life, and leave the soul itself prostrate and powerless beneath the ruins.

There are temptations to indolence ; to peevishness over ingratitude, or over apparent want of success or of appreciation ; to sensual indulgence ; to prostitution of the Lord's work to purposes of ambition. These, and others akin to them, are grave and common dangers. Such

13   s

temptations appeal with Satanic shrewdness to our weakness. Their suggestions seem often so fairly in line with our work; they come so stealthily, in the disguise of " the speech of Salem," — that many a Christian is wrecked by them ere he is aware. He need not be wrecked: he always knows *something* is amiss, before the destruction comes; and yet, now as ever, "Facilis descensus Averni;" the steeps are smooth, and the foot that ventures on them is sure to slip.

There is constant need of searching scrutiny, lest *self* creep in among our motives, to poison the soul and vitiate its labors. " Watch and pray, that ye enter not into temptation; the spirit indeed is willing, but the flesh is weak." " We have this treasure in earthen vessels."

One may always know the prevailing " fashion " in the Adversary's kingdom, by its fruit, the mania of the day. In our time, it is a false charity for the world. This results in a toning down of the Gospel to suit men, and a propping up of the world to an apparent level with the kingdom ; so that the sinews of evangelistic effort are cut : —

" *Cui bono ?* Why shall we be so eager about the *destiny* of men ? God will take care of that: men are very well. The future is distant: the present is upon us. Be practical! Let us see to the *culture* of men."

No worse damage can be done to man, than is thus done. The pure Gospel is the sinner's best friend. The unwelcome truth is what he most needs to hear. The sad facts in his case should be plainly stated, not concealed. They are false friends, lying friends, who " prophesy smooth words " to men, when they and we need the stern, hard, humbling *truth !* " It is no kindness to a drowning man to say that he can swim." Christ said : " He that believeth and is baptized, shall be saved ; but he that believeth not shall be damned." Christians can do no better than take up and repeat the words, often and loud, till the echo rings again ; and in earnest, assured that they are true.

In whatever form the Adversary comes, he

must be met and vanquished;—"Whom resist."
Christ is stronger than Satan, and He is with
us. Satan "will flee." His efforts to hinder
and mar cannot be successful, if the soul stand
firm. Only those who flinch get hurt. The
truest prudence is to fight.

Let no man fear to work for Christ. God
calls. There is a lion in the way, but he is
harmless. There is the appearance of darkness
ahead; but, approaching it, it vanishes before
the *Light.*

III.

MOTIVES.

"I beseech you, therefore, brethren, by the mercies of God."— Rom. xii. 1.

"WILL it pay?"

This is the shape the American question is wont to take. Let us see.

1. *It is God who calls to this service.* Is not God a good paymaster? Can the King act meanly? Royalty is accustomed to be lavish: God is the King of kings. His gifts, so far as shown, are unstinted to a marvel. It is His glory to give on a magnificent scale. He *will* be peerless in His largess. How petty the unbelief that doubts Him!

2. *This service is free.* No one is compelled to it. Withholding it does not forfeit heaven: "The gifts and calling of God are without repentance." "Grace hath no conditions." The soul may serve, or may refuse to serve. God repudiates the service of restraint, of hate, fear,

or barter. He will have nothing that is not purely voluntary, the service of love. There is no compulsion.

3. *This is a service of peculiar and matchless honor.* It is co-operation with Christ, the King: "We are co-workers together with God." Angels are withheld from it, that it may be given to us. The Holy Ghost is restricted — as to His direct operations — to the feeble-minded and the dying children, in order that human agency may have the full field. In this field we have no rivals. To preach the gospel, to ransom the lost, to help the needy, to comfort the afflicted, and even to hasten the coming of the King, make up a work whose instrumentalities are committed solely to the hands of Christians. Ours is the opportunity; and each has his part.

The work is *service*, the most noble of all forms of labor, consecrated by the Master and cast in the mould of God's peculiar method.

It is a devotion to the interests of souls, and to the honor of the King of kings. He who engages in it, has a vastly greater dignity than belongs to the highest official of any human government. The charge of souls is more honorable than the custody of millions of money. The saving one of these souls from death, is greater usefulness than can be attained by the wisest statesmanship or the broadest philanthropy.

How despicable and how trifling, in the comparison, seems the life that is given to the petty strifes, the vanishing attainments, the useless and even hurtful achievements, at which most men aim!

What other work has fruits which pass the limit of the grave? No statesman, as such; no warrior, poet, artist, historian, scientist, or even philanthropist, as such, — can win a fame which shall reach to other worlds and to the ages of eternity; yet the humblest Christian has this boundless reach.

This service is in the employment of the Lord of lords. It calls into action the purest, noblest emotions of the soul, and only those. It puts in our hands, or gives us the co-operation of, all the machinery of time and all the forces of eternity. Its barter is in the ransom of immortal souls, its very currency is more precious than gold, and its rewards are kingdoms.

This is the work of heroes: each worker is a hero. It is the work of Paul; of Huss and Wickliffe; of Luther, Calvin, and Knox; of Whitfield and the Wesleys; of John Howard; and of all the most heroic, the most honored souls whose names are given us. It is the work which ennobled the women of the Bible, Miriam and Esther, Dorcas and Priscilla, and scores of others whose achievements have provoked a hallowed emulation among the Christian women of modern times.

This is labor of the most exalted kind: it is the nearest approach to the work of the Son of God that opens its gates to men. It is not too much to call it an employment of "peculiar and matchless honor;" and by this charm, which Love has lent it, it is legitimately sought to entice men to its activities.

4. *The heart of the Christian demands for him*

a share in this work: "The love of Christ *con-straineth* us."

A traveller was once observed to have the service of an attendant whose strict fidelity and warmth of devotion were manifest. A stranger asked: —

"Why do you serve him? you are free."

"He redeemed me! *He redeemed me!* I want to serve him; I cannot help serving him," was the reply, startling in its emphasis and eagerness.

Christ redeemed the soul. The "carnal mind" may object to serving Him, does object; but the Christian's *self* loves the Redeemer with a pure, unselfish, and unquenchable devotion. If the cries of the soul be not smothered in sin, or drowned by the tumult of earthly care, they will command attention and obedience. Love overrides all difficulties, overleaps all barriers, overcomes all distance. Love longs to serve its Object, and pines if it be denied. Jesus needed to ask Simon Peter, before restoring him to the apostolate, the single question, "Lovest thou

13*

me?" But the one question was thrice repeated.

Work for Christ is the spontaneous impulse of the untrammelled Christian.

5. *There is peculiar and unequalled present pleasure in this work.* It promotes and compels communion with God, lifting the soul into the pure atmosphere of heaven. It brings into pleasing exercise the Christian virtues. It bestows the joy of pleasing others, of helping men; the joy, passing expression, of seeing men *saved*, through one's own exertions; and the joy unspeakable, of pleasing Christ.

6. *There is a reward.* Christ comes again! He will call His disciples together unto Himself. Then : —

" Every man's work shall be made manifest; for the day shall declare it, because it shall be revealed by fire, and the fire shall try every man's work, of what sort it is. If any man's work abide, . . . he shall receive a reward. If any man's work shall be burned, he shall suffer loss; but he himself shall be saved, yet so as by fire."

Salvation is a gift: works are of no avail for the purchase; Christ's work was sufficient. Having received the gift, all we do for Him is for His glory and our profit. If, now, after accepting the " foundation . . . that is laid, which is Jesus Christ," the soul fail to " work ; " or, if the work prove to be but " wood, hay, stubble," and is " burned," — he shall be saved, indeed, but " he shall suffer loss." If the work endure the test, if it prove to be " gold, silver, precious stones," the worker " shall receive a reward."

When the Master shall return to institute this inquiry, no man can tell. The Scriptures say : —

" But of that day, and hour, knoweth no man."

" Watch, therefore, for ye know not what hour your Lord doth come."

" Therefore be ye also ready ; for in such an hour as ye think not the Son of man cometh."

The command is : "Occupy *till* I come."

Christians are wont to miss the realization of these statements and so lose their force, by saying, as did some of old, " My Lord delayeth

His coming;" and "Where is the promise of
His coming? for since the fathers fell asleep all
things continue as they were from the beginning
of the creation."

The plea seems natural, if not necessary; since
already the delay has extended over eighteen
hundred years. Nevertheless, the inspired reproof immediately follows: —

"But, beloved, be not ignorant of this one thing,
that one day is with the Lord as a thousand years,
and a thousand years as one day. The Lord is *not*
slack concerning His promise. . . . But the day of
the Lord will come as a thief in the night. . . .
Wherefore, beloved, *seeing that ye look for such things,*
be diligent, that *ye may be found of Him* in peace,
without spot, and blameless."

7. *The necessities of men clamor for Christian
work.* Humanity needs nothing so much as the
Gospel. Chief among man's woes are these,
which only the gospel of Christ can heal:
his helplessness in affliction; his gloom under
disappointment; his dread of death; his barren-
ness and sinfulness of heart; his soul-cry for the
unknown God; his hopeless yearning for a better

life; his despair of deliverance from lust, from degradation, from a guilty conscience; his condemnation to an eternal hell; and his utter and appalling need of an opened heaven.

This multitude of sorrows is to-day pressing down on the hearts of humanity : wringing from them groans and tears ; driving many to strong drink, some to frenzy, some to crime, some to despair, and some to the suicide's grave. These real, wide-spread, and terrific woes of men *demand* from Christians the extension of the help and healing of the Gospel of Jesus Christ, the Son of God.

8. One last appeal comes, *for the honor of the Cross.* The honor of the Redeemer is at stake, and it suffers many a stain because of the indolence and the indifference of His sworn adherents. Said an infidel to a Christian friend : —

"You do not believe these things yourself."

"I certainly do!"

"You do not, and I can prove it. If I believed, as you say you do, that one of my dearest friends was doomed to hell, liable to sink into it any moment, and in reach of a full salvation which might be had for the taking, do you suppose I would let him alone for weeks at a time? I would give him no peace, day nor night, till he should take the gift. I would din it in his ears perpetually. I would follow him about. I would go out upon the street whenever I should see him passing, take hold of him, stop him, and *compel* him to listen: I could not rest until he should be safe."

Can the *inactive* Christian make any satisfactory reply? The Cross is contemned because of the sloth, the indifference, of those who owe to it their eternal all, and who are sworn to defend its honor and push its claims. There is no escape from the fearful responsibility and the terrific blame.

Further, the honor of the " Name above every name " is irrevocably bound up with the success of this work. The ransomed are to be called out from among men and gathered into the kingdom. The word is to be preached for a witness to all nations. The Gospel is to carry its Light to every corner of the earth, before the eyes of every man, and into the hearts of all the chosen. The Redeemer's word is pledged. The work must be done, — or the Cross proves a failure and a farce! *And on Christians only rests the responsibility of doing it.* Christ, having bought them with His blood and bound them to Himself by the strongest and most endearing ties, has in a manner placed Himself in their hands, committed His honor to their keeping. He has no other agency to employ. The Light must shine: it is appointed that it shall shine through the lives and the labors of the Children of Light.

> " Rise ! for the day is passing,
> And you lie dreaming on !
> The others have buckled their armor,
> And forth to the fight have gone ;
> A place in the ranks awaits you ;
> Each man has some part to play ;
> The past and the future are looking
> In the face of the stern to-day ! "

IV.

WHAT TO DO.

" Whatsoever thy hand findeth to do, do it with thy might." —
Ecc. ix. 10.

WHEN Paul, on his conversion, asked what the Lord would have him do, he was commanded: " Arise, and go into the city, and it shall be told thee what thou must do." The answer is significant.

1. *The thread of life is to be taken up where it has been laid down.* This is the beginning of Christian conduct.

2. *Direction must be sought through the ordinary and appointed agencies.* This is the way to find one's appointed work.

The first thing to be done by the Christian who seeks work, is simply to go on in his present course of life, adding to it a new consecration. It is not necessary or natural, and it is seldom duty, to break off abruptly from former plans and habits, and to change the general conditions of the life. Direction must first be sought from the Light, as Paul was sent to seek it in Damascus, — from Ananias, as God's mouth-piece. This search requires time. Until it shall have been made, and until its fruit be an unmistakable call to something of the kind, no sweeping change should be permitted. At least the framework of present endeavor, must be supplied by past habit. The germ feeds on the decaying matter of the seed : the new life feeds on the dead habit of the old. Retain it ; use it ; and, from the outset, animate it by a new spirit of service.

The contrary course is not uncommon : but it is not Scriptural ; and it is hurtful. It furnishes the clew to many a woful blunder and wretched failure. The new-fledged devotion seeks expression : it goes self-guided, or it is pushed forward by indiscreet friends. Instantly an untried life begins. Even the framework is new ; habits are changed ; study, business, or domestic routine, is rudely sacrificed. The soul is in strange waters. There seems some "freedom " at first. Soon comes restriction; then a misstep; then — a fall!

Almost equally mischievous is the custom of permitting the first flush of desire to pass without making the inquiry for work, and finding the answer accorded. The soul readily relapses into indolence. The eyes new-opened must quickly discover something to enchain and compel attention, or they will close again: they must find some field of work, as well as the Object of faith.

The opportunity that lies nearest, comes first. There is opportunity for a quiet, modest word to a friend; for a new element in correspondence; for a word of sympathy here, or an act of kindness there. Little things, easily done; in places convenient to the daily walk, easily found; with effort easily put forth, even by the new-given, infant strength; in directions easily discerned even by the untrained eye, where there will be little danger of hurtful mistake.

There is much to be done which all may do.

The world would be brighter and better; tears
would be fewer; many a home would be sweetly
robbed of its distress; and many a soul would
be brought to the Master's feet, — if the little
effort possible, here or there, were always freely
made. These are the deeds especially recommended by our Saviour; and each of them is
coupled with a specific promise of reward : —

"I was a hungered, and ye gave me meat; I was
thirsty, and ye gave me drink; I was a stranger, and
ye took me in; naked, and ye clothed me; I was sick,
and ye visited me; I was in prison, and ye came unto
me. . . . Inasmuch as ye have done it unto one of the
least of these my brethren, ye have done it unto me."

"And whosoever shall give to drink unto one of
these little ones a cup of cold water only, in the name
of a disciple, verily I say unto you, he shall in no wise
lose his reward."

The loudest call for work to-day, is upon
those whose spheres are circumscribed, whose
opportunities seem few, whose abilities are limited, whose means are scant, whose speech perhaps is slow, and whose place is humble. It
was only the servant who had but one talent,

who so shamefully neglected his opportunities. So likewise, very often, it is they who can do but little — a trifle here or there for Jesus — who are guilty of the greatest failure. These persons cannot be selected from the mass, for rebuke, as readily as those whose position makes them more prominent. But it scarcely admits of a doubt, when we consider their number and their close contact with those who are in greatest need, that the possibilities of service from people of this class, as a whole, are greater than those of all other classes; and that more hinderance and harm result to the kingdom of Christ from their neglect, than from all other causes combined!

In general, the first call to work for the Master regards the home, the counting-room, the office, the work-shop, the neighborhood, the circle of acquaintance. It regards not extraordinary, but the most ordinary, kinds of work, the work that lies nearest the common conduct, — the word, the act of kindness, the gift of charity, the helping hand, the visit to the sick, the call in Christ's name on a godless neighbor or companion. And "He that is faithful in that which is least, is faithful also in much."

Further, however; *there is need of a larger co-operation with those already at work*, in the agencies already in operation. The work of the Sunday school is calling for help, often in vain, upon those whose interests and opportunities lie very near it. Their presence is needed; their endeavor to bring others; their thought; their prevision and their provision; their aid to the spirituality of tone, and to the thoroughness of work, which our Sunday schools often lack; and their exertions to extend the influence of this important agency of the church. This work cannot be done by proxy, as so many seem to suppose.

The endeavor to induce men to attend divine service is much needed; to make them "feel at home" when there, so that they will come again; to attach men to the church by legitimate means, which always bind most strongly; to make the church a channel of grace to men whom it does not reach, and whom it should reach.

Every cause of benevolence, every agency of evangelism, education, and charity, needs help. Our countless societies, seminaries, colleges, schools of theology, are continually struggling for life ; or, at best, for a more vigorous life. Who will help ?   There are almost innumerable agencies already in operation, all of them deriving their existence and authority in some way from the church of Jesus Christ.   The field for help is limitless.   Willing hands, ready speech, scheming brains, and open purses, are in demand. When shall they be laid on the Redeemer's altar ?

Beyond all this, there are needed *new agencies of organized effort ;* and new channels for individual endeavor and beneficence are open — to eyes that are ready to discern them.   The number passes reckoning ; the variety forbids delineation.

There is room for men (and women !) of one idea.   The temperance cause needs them.   The prisoners need them. The ignorant and the unevangelized need them. New lines of labor. New channels of giving. New subjects for thought, plan, and prayer. New objects of life!

Reforms are to be instituted, and others abetted. The Gospel is to be preached, printed, circulated, recommended. The poor are to be fed. The fallen are to be lifted up. The weak are to be strengthened.

The work is large. There is plenty of room for various tastes and capabilities. The field is the world. The command of the Master is, "Go!" Go to help, to heal, to save, among thirteen hundred millions of men, *anywhere!* The vast majority of this teeming multitude are ignorant, vicious, and LOST! and all of them are suffering. The harvest is plenteous, — but the laborers are few! The prayer ascends from many an aching heart, in distant echo of the Master's cry, "Send forth more LABORERS into the harvest." Time presses. Needs crowd. Christ commands, "Go, work." "Whatsoever thy hand findeth to do, do it with thy might."

Let the Children of Light make haste to put on the armor of Light.

" Go, labor on ; spend and be spent,
 Thy joy to do the Master's will ;
It is the way the Master went :
 Should not the servant tread it still ?

" Go, labor on ! 'Tis not for naught ;
 Thine earthly loss is heavenly gain ;
Men heed thee, love thee, praise thee not :
 The Master praises ; — what are men ?

" Go, labor on ! Enough, while here,
 If He shall praise thee ; if He deign
Thy willing heart to mark and cheer :
 No toil for Him shall be in vain.

" Toil on ! and in thy work rejoice ;
 For toil, comes rest ; for exile, home.
Soon shalt thou hear the Bridegroom's voice,
 The midnight peal : ' *Behold*, I COME ! ' "

Cambridge : Press of John Wilson & Son.

www.ingramcontent.com/pod-product-compliance
Lightning Source LLC
Chambersburg PA
CBHW020952030726
47496CB00005B/1471